COLONY TWO MARS

A SCIENCE FICTION THRILLER

GERALD M. KILBY

OUTER PLANET
MEDIA

For notifications on upcoming books, and access to my FREE starter library, please join my Readers Group at www.geraldmkilby.com.

CONTENTS

MOON BASE DELTA

Solar Storm

Resource Control

Power Vacuum

THE BELT

Entanglement

Entropy

Evolution

Enigma

Exodus

Emergence

COLONY MARS

Colony One Mars

Colony Two Mars

Colony Three Mars

Jezero City

Surface Tension

Plains of Utopia

TECHNOTHRILLER

Chain Reaction

Brain Gain

SHORT STORIES

Gizmo Origin

Winds of Mars

1

THE ANIMAL

D r. Jann Malbec stood a little over knee-deep at the edge of the pond in the biodome of Colony One. She was still and quiet, her face to the sun so as not to cast a shadow over its surface and frighten the fish. She held a spear high above her shoulder and waited. After a while the fish would start to swim around her legs, sometimes even touching her. Jann held fast until the right moment and then loosed the spear. It knifed through the water, bending in the refracted light.

Damn, only one, she thought as she pulled it out. Her record was two in one throw, three was exponentially more difficult to achieve. The fish flapped and squirmed on the stick as she stepped out and brought it over to the campfire she had set up on the central dais. Grabbing the fish by the tail, she slid it off the spear and whacked its head on the hard floor to kill it and stop it flapping around. From a small mound of dry kindling Jann grabbed a handful of straw, placed it on the dying embers and blew gently to get it going again. Soon it was burning steady. It crackled and sparked as she threw more kindling on.

Sitting down cross-legged, she started to gut the fish with a sharp knife that she kept on a belt around her waist. The area around her was covered in the scattered remains of similar meals she had eaten in this place. As soon as the fish was cleaned she skewered it and set it on the fire to cook. Then she sat back and waited, turning it every so often to prevent the flesh from blackening.

Through the dense foliage all around her she could hear the robot going about its business: harvesting, maintaining, monitoring. She didn't speak to it much these days. It didn't seem to mind—it was a robot after all. In the beginning it was different, she had had long conversations with it. But after a while she grew tired of the rhetorical analysis of its dialog. The robot simply took in what she said, analyzed it and regurgitated it back in a reorganized form. It was like talking to a distorted mirror. Sometimes she even got angry at it, and banished it from her space. Then after a while, oddly, she would feel guilty and would seek it out again. How strange is the human spirit to feel empathy for a machine. Now though, she left it to its work. It managed the colony and there really wasn't much Jann had to do. The colony didn't need her input, it just needed the robot.

. . .

AFTER THE CATACLYSMIC events of the ill-fated ISA Mars mission, Dr. Jann Malbec ended up being the only survivor. Nonetheless, since the Mars Ascent Vehicle (MAV) was still intact, she had a possible way home. Mission control had sent her details on how to fabricate new fuel tanks after the originals had been destroyed when she had immolated Annis Romanov in a fiery ball of rocket fuel. Jann and the robot had set about building these, but when they were ready, she had a new problem. As far as the ISA was concerned, she was still a potential biohazard, a Typhoid Mary, so to speak. They would not let her return unless she could prove she was not a contaminant.

So Jann worked to gain some understanding of the bacteria that had devastated the ISA mission, and Commander Decker in particular. But try as she might she simply did not possess the equipment to gain any further understanding. In the end she simply gave up. And with it, any hope of using the MAV to return to Earth. She had no option but to wait it out until the next ISA mission. The colony was self-sustaining and well resourced, so she was in no real danger.

But as the first year passed, messages from mission control started to include phrases such as: budget constraints, political apathy, low priority. Fear grew in Jann's mind that Earth was losing its appetite for Mars. It became clear to her that there was little desire, by any of the ISA member governments, to spend billions rescuing someone who could potentially devastate the entire population of the planet. So they had effectively abandoned her.

At the start she was angry, but as the second year passed she began to accept it. She couldn't blame them, really. By the third year, she had resigned herself to dying on Mars. The only problem was, like Nills, she was getting younger, not older. To die on Mars might take her a very, very long time. Unless it was by her own hand—and she began to realize it might come to that in the end.

So day by day, slowly but surely, the colony had changed her and made Dr. Jann Malbec just another part of its enormous biological ecosystem. It needed a human to complete its collection of flora and fauna, so it entered deep into her psyche and sought out the essence of the animal that lay within. By now, she wore little clothing and went barefoot. Her food she hunted by spear and gathered by hand. She ate by the fire and slept in a tree. Her hair had become a long mass of matted dreadlocks. The colony had claimed her for itself—and it had done a good job.

She had made herself a nest high up in the crown of the tallest coconut tree, and at night, looked out through the translucent dome roof at the vastness of the universe. What was she becoming? An exotic specimen in an equally exotic enclosure, to be peered at by the gods? Sometimes she would rise from her bed of straw and leaves and shake her fists at the heavens. She would rant and rage against her sense of insignificance and challenge the infinity of the void above her, like King Lear going mad on the mountain. "Screw you, space!" or words to that effect.

LIFTING the skewered fish from the fire, Jann set it down on a banana leaf to cool. She couldn't hear the robot anymore, it must have moved off to tend to some other part of the biodome. While she waited for her meal to cool she lifted up the spear and examined the point. It had become blunt with use; she would set about sharpening it later. Jann had become quite adept with it. She had taken to setting up targets in and around the biodome and would run through as fast as she could firing off spears, one after the other as she flew by. By now, she seldom missed. Once she got so angry at the robot she threw one at it. She missed that time.

Jann tested the fish; it was ready. She clamped the skewer between her teeth and scampered up the trunk of the tall coconut tree to her nest, where she could relax and eat her meal. From its height she had a commanding view over the whole biodome canopy. It felt safe. She had just finished the last of her meal and was wiping her face with the back of her hand when she heard the robot enter the biodome again. From the sound, it was moving at speed. It burst through the dense foliage out onto the central dais, stopped, scanned the area, and then tilted its head up at Jann.

"GO AWAY!" she shouted at it.

"Dr. Malbec, there is something important you need to know."

"I don't want to know, now go away." She picked up a coconut and flung it at the little robot. It didn't dodge, it simply caught it in its metal hand. It had uncanny reflexes. Jann was always impressed at how it could do this. Sometimes she would sneak up behind it and fire off a spear. It nearly always caught it. The only time it didn't was when it had calculated that whatever projectile Jann was throwing at it was going to miss. Jann had no idea how it could be so accurate and agile. But then again, it was a machine.

It placed the coconut gently on the ground. "Jann, this is important. Do I have your attention?"

Jann glared at it. "Oh, all right, what is it?"

"Another Earthling has just entered the airlock."

Jann felt like she had been physically kicked in the gut. She had to sit down.

"Jann, did you hear what I said?"

She tried to get words out of her mouth but they just wouldn't come.

"Jann?"

"That... that's... not... possible." She thought maybe the robot was playing a trick on her, getting its own back for her insensitivity and borderline cruelty to it. But it was a droid, it was straight and true, and in many respects, a better friend to her than many humans she had known.

"Okay... I need to think... I need to..." her sentence trailed off.

"I understand that this is an improbable event. But nonetheless, another Earthling has entered the airlock."

"How can this be?"

"I possess insufficient data to offer any useful analysis. What do you want me to do?"

Jann thought about this. "Can it get in?"

"It is a he, and he is already in. However, he cannot move as he appears to be barely alive."

Jann's shock was beginning to recede, enough for her to gain some control. "Okay, okay, I'm coming." She clambered down the tree trunk, slowly, as she was still shaken by this news. Near the base she jumped down onto the dais, grabbed her spear and ran off towards the main airlock. "Come on, Gizmo, let's see this Earthling."

JANN LOOKED at the forlorn figure lying on the floor of the airlock with a sense of incredulity. "Where in God's name did he come from?"

"That is a very good question, Jann," replied Gizmo.

She inched closer, still holding the spear high, just in case. But it was clear this human was no threat. He had passed out and his life was ebbing away. She put down the spear and knelt beside him. His suit was battered and filthy. Patched up to maintain its integrity and mechanically hacked to make it function. It was more steampunk than space age. But she could still make out it was from the colony.

"He's a colonist, judging by the design of the suit. Quick, help me get him in to the medlab."

With that, Gizmo lifted the unconscious figure and brought him out of the airlock. They placed him on the table in the medlab, removed his suit and hooked up several IVs to get fluids into him as quickly as possible. His body had lost its ability to sweat and his core temperature was critically high.

"He's dangerously dehydrated; he could have a heart attack any minute."

After some time, Jann had managed to stabilize him. "Who the hell is he?"

"We could do a retinal scan and see if we get a match from the medlab database," offered Gizmo.

"Okay, let's do that. Then at least we might get some clues." Jann tapped a few buttons on the operating table control panel and an arm extended from the wall, positioning itself over his head. A thin line of light scanned across his face as Jann deftly pushed back one of his eyelids. Data began to display on the main monitor. As it searched, images of colonists momentarily flashed on screen, then it stopped. It had found a match. Thomas Boateng. Colonist number 27.

Jann read the data. "This can't be right."

"It has a 99.9% accuracy probability," said Gizmo.

"Well this must be in the 0.1% range because it says this colonist died over seven years ago."

"Intriguing," replied Gizmo. "I assume you mean Earth years?"

"It says here that he died on sol 6,348, due to a severe brain aneurysm as the result of injuries sustained in a mining accident." She looked back at the patient. "So this guy must be someone else."

"He cannot be someone else, the retinal scan is very accurate."

"Well he can't be dead and alive at the same time."

"Indeed. That would be very unlikely."

The bio-monitor screeched an alarm as the colonist's vitals went critical. "Dammit, he's going into cardiac arrest. Quick, get the defibrillator." Jann started ripping off the remaining clothes around the colonist's chest as Gizmo handed her the pads. She rubbed them together to get an even coating of gel and positioned them on his upper ribcage. "Clear." She hit the button and several hundred volts tore through his body. His back arched for a moment then he slumped back down. The alarm continued. "Shit, come on." Jann waited for the charge to build and tried again, and again, and again.

HIS SKIN WAS SCORCHED and there was a distinct smell of burning flesh in the air. But no joy. Jann flicked the switch on the bio-monitor to silence the alarm. He was still. She stood back and looked at the colonist. "Well, he's dead now, for sure. We may never know who he was."

"He is Thomas Boateng."

"He can't be, Gizmo." Jann was beginning to get angry at its infuriating rationality, so she distracted herself by scanning through the medical records of the dead colonist. They were extensive. "It says here he should have a benign mole just above the left shoulder blade." She glanced over at Gizmo. "Let's take a look."

They raised him up and peeled away the remains of his tattered vest. "Holy crap," Jann was stunned.

"It seems this really is Boateng." Gizmo lowered the body down again.

"That's just not possible."

"It is not probable. But as you so rightly pointed out to me many years ago, it would seem it is, indeed, possible. Here lies the evidence." Gizmo extended a mechanical arm towards the dead man with all the theater of a stage artist.

"There's one way to find out for sure and that's do a dental x-ray." Jann tapped a few buttons on the operating table control panel and a large doughnut-shaped ring started to advance along the table. It moved across the face of the dead colonist and the resultant scan rendered on the main screen. Jann now tapped the historical image from the dental records and the two images were presented together. "That's weird."

"What is?" said Gizmo.

"Well I'm no expert at dental forensics but the shape and layout of the teeth and jaw are identical. Except this guy hasn't had any dental work, not even a filling."

"Is that strange?"

"Yes, very. If I were to hazard a guess I would say this is a younger version of the same person."

"Like Nills?"

"Yes and no. Nills was getting younger, that's correct. But this guy would seem to have come back from the dead." She went silent for a moment. "The other big question is where did he come from?"

"The only possible place is the mining outpost, on the far side of the crater."

"That's a hell of a long walk."

"Indeed. Probably why he died in the attempt."

"But Nills said no one in the mine survived."

"It would seem Nills was wrong."

"Holy shit, maybe there are more people out there?"

"It is a distinct possibility."

Jann turned and rubbed her head. "I need time to think, this is all too much. For someone to show up like that after all this time is one thing. But the fact that this person already died seven years ago is... I don't know... mind blowing."

"There is something we could do to shed some light on the mystery."

"What's that?"

"Pay a visit to the mausoleum."

"You mean see if the original body of Boateng is still there?"

"Exactly."

"If it is, then what?"

"Then that means there are two Thomas Boatengs, impossible as that may be."

JANN SWITCHED off the main screen and stopped short as she caught her reflection in the blank monitor. She stared at herself in shock. Instead of Dr. Jann Malbec, Science Officer of the ISA Mars mission, what returned her gaze was a semi-naked, feral animal. Was this what she had become? "Christ, is that actually me?" She looked away. Maybe I truly have gone mad. Then a thought shook her to her very core. "How would I really know?"

She walked out of the medlab, making sure to lock the door. It was done out of paranoia, from the memories of what had happened there before. Then she did something she hadn't done in a very long time. She went and had a shower.

2

MORE THAN ONE

Jann sat in her wicker chair in the central dais wearing a crisp clean Colony One jumpsuit, which itched. She examined her thick matted hair in a small mirror as Gizmo waited silently beside her. "If I'm going to EVA out to the mausoleum my head is not going to fit in a helmet with all this hair. Will you cut it for me, Gizmo?"

"Certainly, Jann. How would you like it?"

"Just take it all off. Leave about a centimeter."

Gizmo moved closer, selected a suitable tool from its collection and went to work. It took only a few minutes for Jann's matted hair to form a large mound on the floor of the dais. When Gizmo finished she examined the robot's handiwork in the mirror. She rubbed her hand over her scalp and felt the tight crop. It was like a velvet mat. "Oh, that feels so much better. My head must be a few kilos lighter."

GERALD M. KILBY

"My pleasure, I am here to assist."

"Okay then, let's go do this. Let's see if there really are two Thomas Boatengs."

THE MAUSOLEUM WAS FASHIONED from an old lander module and isolated from the main Colony One structure. It had no power or life support. There was no need for that in a place for the dead. Jann cracked the handle on the makeshift crypt and swung the door open. She stepped inside and scanned the racks. Paolio, Lu, Kevin... they were all here, the entire crew of the doomed ISA mission. It even housed what was left of Annis. A blackened husk was all that remained after Jann had incinerated her.

This module had been used by the original colonists as a place to temporarily store the dead before they were buried. But as time passed, they realized that in the rarefied atmosphere of Mars, bodies do not decompose. So they simply left them interred in here. As more dead were added it became the de facto mausoleum for Colony One.

The walls were lined with horizontal metal racks, floor to ceiling. On these lay the corpses of the departed. In the center was a raised circular table, holding artifacts of faith and no faith, as well as totems of remembrance. Jann considered that in some distant time, it might become a hallowed place. Venerated by the future citizens of Mars as a direct link to their foundation history.

She moved over to where the body of Thomas Boateng should be resting. It was still there, lying on a long metal shelf. A thin layer of dust had accumulated over it; it had been there a long time. She looked at the desiccated face. It was hard to be sure, but there was a vague resemblance to the recently deceased visitor. She judged this simply by a visual inspection of body height and facial structure rather than from anything scientific. Jann then considered looking for the mole on his shoulder but now that she was face to face, she couldn't bring herself to disturb the dead.

"*Satisfied?*" Gizmo's voice resonated in her helmet as the robot buzzed in beside her.

"Yes and no. If this guy died seven years ago, then who is the person on the operating table in the medlab?"

"*It is another Thomas Boateng.*"

"I find that very hard to comprehend." She sighed. "Come on, let's go. There's nothing more we can do here." They moved outside and Jann swung the door closed. Hopefully she would not have to visit this place again anytime soon.

IN THE EARLY days of her life in Colony One, Jann had always considered the mine as an area needing more detailed investigation. A place where she might find some answers. But it was considerably farther than Nills had originally suggested—over thirty kilometers away on the other side of the Jezero crater. Much too far to EVA, as the dead colonist had found out to his detriment. So she had given the mine no further thought. Now, though, it seemed that it was not as dead as Nills had led her to believe—*something* was going on over there. Yet, even if she could not EVA to it, she could at least start to look in the Colony One archives and get a better understanding of its formation, and perhaps even its true purpose. So it was a reinvigorated Jann that set to work in the operations room in Colony One.

MUCH OF WHAT was contained in the archives was vague and sparse. Most of what Jann had learned had come from Nills. She knew that the early colonists had discovered a mineral rich cave system on the other side of the crater rim. This much was common knowledge. She also knew that at some point, it had been sealed up and a pressurized atmosphere created inside. This allowed it to be used not just as a mine but also as a secondary colony —Colony Two.

Food production had been established inside and, over time, many of the original colonists had moved over there permanently. Nills intimated that this had been as a direct response to the increasing invasiveness of the reality TV model that had funded the initial colony. But what was of most interest to Jann was the fact that the geneticists had also relocated there, shortly before everything went to rat shit in Colony One.

She stood up from the workstation terminal and stretched her shoulders. She had been studying the archives for over three hours straight but had not learned anything she didn't know already. She rubbed her head again; it was becoming a habit. She liked the feel of her closely cropped skull and the lightness it gave her. She moved over to the newly repaired holo-table. The original had been damaged when the insane Commander Decker threw Paolio at it. Every time Jann used it she couldn't help but shed a tear for her dear friend. Her feelings for Decker were not quite the same. But in reality, he was just as much a victim as any of the others of the unfortunate ISA crew.

She brought up a map of the crater and zoomed out to get a broad view. It rendered itself in 3D so she could get a sense of the scale of the vast crater. Jann rotated it and found the location of the mining outpost. It was at least thirty-five kilometers away. *That's a hell of a walk to undertake in a battered EVA suit*, she thought. She zoomed in on the site and a wire-frame image of the structure began to render as it dialed in closer. It was big. Maybe twenty times the volume of Colony One, and that could accommodate a hundred people. But the wire-frame was sketchy, there was very little detail in it.

Jann looked up as Gizmo entered the operations room. "Gizmo. Have a look at this." She pointed to the location of Colony Two on the holo-table. "How come there's so little detail on the internal structure of the mine?"

Gizmo moved closer and examined it. "It does seem very incomplete."

"From my analysis there should be areas for food production, accommodation, operation, processing and a whole bunch of other stuff. But this is minimal."

"They obviously were not too interested in updating the data."

"Or they were trying to hide its true nature." She sighed and looked at Gizmo.

"Did you move the body?"

"Yes, he is now lying beside himself in the mausoleum."

"You're assuming that they are the same person, Gizmo."

"I never assume, Jann."

"Well, if you're correct—and let's face it, you always are—then that would mean only one thing. That this guy must be a clone."

"A genetically identical human?" said Gizmo.

"Yes."

"Interesting."

"What's even more interesting, Gizmo, is there are probably a lot more."

3

IN SEARCH OF ANSWERS

Jann sat in a battered armchair in the common room of Colony One. It was the first time she had done so in over a year. The table before her was laid out with dishes and utensils, as well as an ample array of food, all extracted from deep-freeze storage. She had not eaten like this in a very long time, she'd given up on such formal niceties. But, like a ship's captain of old on the far side of the world, taking tea from a fine china tea set, she felt she needed to reconnect with civilized behavior, lest she forget forever.

But it brought with it painful memories of friends long dead, of Paolio, Nills, Lu and Kevin. She raised her cup of colony cider. "Here's to you all," she said, in the memory of all those that she had lost.

Gizmo entered. "Is the food to your liking, Jann?"

"It feels weird, eating off a plate."

"Sorry, but I would not know."

Jann smiled at the quirky robot. "The food's fine, Gizmo. But it would be nice to share it with some friends."

"Well, if it is any consolation, I do enjoy your company."

She laughed. "Thank you, Gizmo. I know I can be difficult. It hasn't been easy for me... this last while."

"That is okay, you are only human after all."

Jann cocked an eyebrow at it. "Coming from a robot I'm not sure how to take that."

"Consider it a compliment."

"All right. I will." She raised her glass to Gizmo and nodded, then sat back. "Tell me, Gizmo, what are my chances of returning to Earth?" It was the same question she had asked of it a hundred times before. Whenever any new message came in from mission control, or when she gained some new insight into the bacteria, she asked this very same question of Gizmo, hoping that this new snippet of data would prompt a different response. It never did. Its reply was always the same. *'None,'* it would say. She understood that in Gizmo's lexicon, this meant anything with less than a 0.01% probability. But this time its response was different.

"Slim. Approximate probability of 2.7%."

Jann nearly choked on her drink. "Slim? How come? What's changed?"

"Quite a lot, Jann. Consider this: you can return to Earth anytime you want, your launch craft is still functioning and the new fuel tanks are ready. The only thing that is preventing you is the need to convince the ISA that you are no longer a biohazard. And the only way you can do that is to find a way to kill it."

"Well, since the research lab is destroyed I have no way to do that. The medlab equipment is not up to the mark for that kind of analysis. Anyway, you know all this, Gizmo."

"True, but what is different, is you may find something in Colony Two. It would seem from our visitor that this is still viable for human life support. And judging by his genetic makeup it would be reasonable to suggest that they have, or had, significant research facilities there."

"I don't know, Gizmo. Even if I was willing to take the risk of exploring it I have no way to get there and back again. An EVA suit just doesn't have the resources."

"You could take the exploration rover."

Jann sat back in her seat and rubbed a hand across her skull. "The rover. I had completely forgotten about that."

TOWARDS THE END of the first year of Jann's isolation in Colony One she was running out of projects to keep her mind focused. The tanks had been built and her efforts at gaining further insight into the malignant bacteria were growing ever more frustrating, hampered as she was by the lack of adequate equipment. This, coupled with the increasingly vague communication from Earth as to a

GERALD M. KILBY

date for the next mission, had prompted Jann to finally explore the derelict sectors of the great colony. It was, after all, the initial mission brief. So since she was going to be stuck here for a while, she might as well get on with it. She also considered that she might find something useful: another lab, or some scientific equipment that she could use.

It was during one of these excursions that she came across the old Colony One exploration rover. It was parked up inside a small derelict workshop dome on the western side of the facility, accessible only by EVA. It was one of two such vehicles, the other, it was assumed, was over in the mining outpost. The rover was non-operational, and had been for five or more years. Jann thought about trying to get it working again, but as time moved on, and her sense of abandonment and isolation increased, her excursions outside became fewer and fewer. By the early part of her second year she had given up on EVA altogether. So, as the colony tightened its grip on her psyche, she retreated into the biodome and spent more and more of her time with the garden: researching it, tending it, becoming one with it. By the close of the second year, not only did she not EVA, she seldom even left the biodome.

"BUT IT'S NOT OPERATIONAL, it hasn't been for a very long time, Gizmo."

"It could be made to function again."

Jann rubbed her hand across the top of her skull again, slowly this time. "I don't know."

"What do you not know?"

Jann sighed. "Even if we do get it working, I'm not sure I want to risk trying to go out there. It's been a long time... for me."

"Yes, it would be an uncertain venture with a high probability of death."

"Thanks, Gizmo, That's very comforting."

"My pleasure, I am here to assist."

"The other big question is: what would I find when, and if, I get there?"

"Unfortunately, I do not have access to sufficient data to give you any useful analysis. However, if Thomas Boateng made it here that would suggest there is life support. So there is a high probability of other life within its confines."

"But if there is, then why have we not heard from them before now?"

"I would suggest a few obvious scenarios: they had no way to communicate or exit the mine. In essence, they were trapped."

"Maybe, but if there are survivors over there the next question is, are they friendly?"

"One would assume that they would be glad of rescue."

"You really think so?"

"It is merely one of many possibilities. They may

equally have descended into a barbarous cohort of violent animals who eat their young."

Jann sighed. "So what you're saying, Gizmo, is you really don't know."

"Too many possible outcomes to predict with any accuracy. The only way you will know for sure is to go there and see. In the meantime I suggest your best course of action would be to revitalize the exploration rover so you have transport should you decide to investigate Colony Two."

Jann thought for a moment, then stood up. "Okay, I suppose there wouldn't be any harm in taking a look at this rover again."

"Very little."

"All right, let's check it out and see if it can be salvaged. Then we can decide."

THE GARAGE WORKSHOP, where the rover was housed, was on the far side of the Colony One site. There was no internal route to it, as the derelict areas had been sealed off a long time ago. Venturing into any of these sectors could be dangerous; they were structurally unsound. So the safest way to get there was to EVA. Jann checked her suit for power and resources as Gizmo waited patiently in the airlock. Being a robot it had no need for life support, it could go anywhere, limited only by the range of its power cell. Jann donned her helmet. It felt strange, now that she had very short hair. It had a roomier feel to it, more like wearing a dome than a helmet. She locked it in place and pressurized the suit. All biometric readings were clear, ready to go.

They worked their way around the perimeter of the facility until they finally reached the workshop. It was a small domed structure with its roof still intact. Along the exterior wall a large airlock protruded, big enough to fit a small truck. They brought a small remote power pack with them and Gizmo set about fiddling with the door's control panel. After a few minutes it had reduced it to a gaping hole of sprouting wires. *"Okay, here goes,"* it said as the door slowly rose up from the ground and slid into the roof. Jann was surprised by how much it looked and worked like a standard garage door. Then again, it was probably a very good design to begin with. The airlock was empty, save for another door at the far end. They moved inside and a short while later Gizmo got it open. They finally entered into the large workshop, and parked in the middle of the space was a six-wheeled, pressurized exploration rover. Jann rubbed her gloved hand along its side. "Well, looks like it's still here."

Over the course of the next few weeks Jann and Gizmo worked to restore power and life support to the maintenance workshop. But Jann still had to EVA to get access to it. They simply did not have the resources to rebuild the damaged structures linking it through to the main facility. All this activity was building up a new routine in Jann's life and imbuing it with a new sense of purpose, and as the sols passed, she felt herself becoming more and more reconnected with reality.

THE ROVER itself was powered by a methane internal combustion engine, the same fuel used for the MAV. It was old school, but made a lot of sense as the fuel could be manufactured easily on Mars. This also gave the machine a great deal of power. It was built to be a tough exploration vehicle with a range of over two hundred kilometers and a fully loaded top speed of sixty-five kilometers per hour. It could also accommodate six crew for a full thirty hours.

It took them another few weeks to get it to a point where they were ready to try and start it up. Jann sat in the driver's seat and surveyed the controls. It had a pretty basic joystick mechanism. The instrument panel was well laid out and clearly defined. It had obviously been designed so that even an idiot could drive it. That suited her just fine. She hit the power on switch. The instrument panel flickered into life, alerts flashed and data started to scroll down the main screen. Gizmo examined it. "Okay, looks like the main systems are operational. Time to see if it will start."

Jann pushed the start button and the rover engine burst into life. She looked over at Gizmo and gave the little droid a thumbs up. She let it run for a minute or two before killing the engine. Gizmo scanned the data readouts on the main screen. "You have fuel for approximately one hundred and eighty kilometers and oxygen for eight hours, twenty-seven minutes." It tilted its head at Jann. "I would say you are good to go, although I would advocate taking it for a test drive, first."

Jann sat back in the driver's seat. "So now I have a decision to make."

"Looks that way."

"Okay, let's get back. Nothing more we can do here this sol. I need to think."

IT TOOK Jann just one night of sleeping in her tree, staring at the stars, to finally make up her mind. To remain in Colony One was a route to insanity, of that she was certain. She was not Nills—she was not that mentally tough. The three years Jann had spent here had already eroded her sense of reality. She had only been brought back from the brink by this new sense of purpose. So she needed to go, not simply because she might find some answers, but because she would find none by staying here.

After several more sols of tests the rover was finally ready for the journey. It was agreed that Gizmo would stay behind and maintain the colony. Not that the little robot wouldn't be useful to her on this trip, but she was worried that some critical system might fail in her absence and there would be no one here to deal with it. The last thing she needed would be to return only to find her primary life support had succumbed to some

GERALD M. KILBY

catastrophe. She was confident there was nothing Gizmo couldn't handle in her absence.

JANN HAD MADE her decision and the moment had come. She clambered on board the exploration rover and, after a last systems check, she signaled for Gizmo to open the airlock. She started up the machine and waved at the little droid as the rover rumbled out of Colony One, and onto the barren planet's surface.

"*Good luck.*" Gizmo's voice resonated from the cabin speaker.

"Thanks," she replied as she pushed the throttle forward. The rover responded, picking up speed.

"*For what it is worth, Jann, your probability of returning to Earth just increased to 7.3%.*"

4

COLONY TWO

The mining outpost was thirty-five kilometers northeast of her, so at a gentle twenty kph she would be there in less than two hours. That gave her plenty of time to investigate and still be able to make the return journey. She passed the solar array field and the old supply lander, and moved on towards the vast expanse of the central crater basin. It reminded her of her first days on the planet, when she went for a walk, testing out one of the small utility rovers they had brought with them. Back then she had felt a strong urge to just keep walking before Lu Chan called her back. Now, that same desire surged within her—to head out into the emptiness and just keep going. Maybe it was the years spent cooped up in Colony One or maybe it was something more primal. Either way, it was exhilarating. Jann opened up the throttle a little more and the rover replied, giving her a new sense of speed and purpose as it accelerated. She hit forty-five kph before she calmed down and let caution prevail. It was not a good plan to push it to breaking point and be stranded out here. She eased back and settled into a safe and steady twenty kph. It was Sunday driving, Martian style.

After an hour or so she began to make out the top of the crater rim on the far side of the basin. It grew in size and clarity as she moved closer. She checked her range and location on the main screen. Another thirty minutes and she would be there. According to the maps and diagrams she had studied back in the colony, the main mine entrance should be located at the base of a tall overhang in the cliff wall. This would make it hard to find without the aid of an accurate chart. Since there was no GPS or magnetic north on Mars, her calculations were done the old fashioned way, by simple trigonometry.

But she wasn't planning on using the main entrance. If one colonist was still alive then there could be others. She didn't want to announce her arrival before checking the place out first, and that meant finding other possible ways in. These were smaller airlocks, dotted farther up the crater rim, and could be accessed on foot. They were installed as escape routes for miners should there be a collapse at the main entrance. She would try one of these first. Hopefully sneak in and do some clandestine reconnaissance.

The crater rim rose up before her. Jann scanned the horizon looking for a natural valley carved out of the cliff. That should be where the main entrance was located. But it was hard to make out in the haze. She had to find it quickly and not spend too much time driving along the base of the cliff. She was pretty sure she was on the right course when eventually she spotted the dip in the crater rim. She aimed for it and stepped on the gas. The rover obliged.

It still took her quite a while to find it. The main entrance was so well concealed she was only three hundred meters away when she spotted it. She slammed on the brakes and came to a skidding halt. Jann waited for the dust to settle before utilizing the onboard camera to scan along the base of the crater's rim. When she found the entrance she zoomed in.

It consisted of one large airlock and two smaller ones. There was nothing out of the ordinary about them other than they were well hidden. She looked at it for a while, half expecting it to open and empty out a cohort of stormtroopers. But it was still and silent—and just a little ominous. Jann started up the rover again and moved off towards the cover of a large rock formation. She parked out of sight of the entrance and switched off the engine.

"Okay, old girl, this is it. Time to focus."

She snapped on her helmet, checked her biometrics and made her way through the airlock at the back of the rover, out onto the surface. The sun was high in the sky and she dimmed her visor to counter the glare. According to the charts, about half a kilometer left of the main entrance there should be a path of sorts, leading up the side of the crater rim for about a hundred meters to a wide ledge; the location of an emergency airlock.

She moved slowly, all the time endeavoring to stay behind whatever cover she could find. But after a few hundred meters the rock formation came to an end and she had no option but to cross to the base in full view. As she worked her way west the cliff face become less sheer and started to slope outward. The ground underfoot also became more rugged and broken as she picked her way between boulders and rocks that had crumbled down the side of the rim over the eons.

Then she saw them. At first she wasn't sure, but as she came closer there was no doubt. She was looking at a trail of footprints coming down the side of the crater and heading off in to the central wasteland. They were crisp and clean, clearly made recently. *The colonist,* she thought. *This is where he came out.* She followed the line of footprints back up the slope. There were places where she lost them over rocky terrain but managed to pick them up again as she progressed upwards. She was high above the level of the crater basin when she saw the entrance. Jann expected to see an airlock but instead it was a low tunnel carved out of the rock, the trail of footprints leading into it. She kept moving, ever upward, towards the tunnel.

THE TUNNEL WAS DARK, but thankfully short, only a few meters deep. At the end was an airlock, and judging by the illumination coming from the control panel, it was functioning. She advanced to face the door. A ripple of fear cascaded through her as she examined the panel. She pressed the *open* button and stood back. The door silently moved inward to reveal a surprisingly large area. It had an inner door at the far end but, oddly, two other doors on either side. Jann considered there might be several routes into this airlock from the mine. It made sense, as this was an escape hatch, presumably for emergencies. She stepped in. The floor was dusty but she could make out the footprints, heading from the door at the far end. She decided this would be her exit. The outer door swung closed and the airlock began to pressurize. Due to its large internal volume it took somewhat longer that the one back in the colony. Jann waited anxiously. She was committed, no going back now. Finally the light went green and there was a momentary pause before the inner door opened.

FOUR PEOPLE STOOD at the entrance, in full hazmat suits. Jann froze as two of them rushed forward and grabbed her arms, pinning them behind her back. She struggled and kicked, but the bulky EVA suit made it difficult to move. They looped a metal band around her waist and she could feel it pulled tight, trapping her arms. She twisted and tried to pull them out, but it was no use.

When they were satisfied she was secured, a third person advanced. He reached up and unfastened her helmet, pulling it off her head. "Get me out of this," she shouted as she kicked out at her assailant, aiming for his groin. But she was too clumsy, and he sidestepped her easily. He raised an arm and Jann could see he held a small syringe. Jann struggled but the two others had a firm grip on her. She felt the needle jab into her neck. "Bastards," she managed, before all consciousness drained out of her.

5

INCARCERATION

Consciousness came to her in waves of ever increasing clarity: light, sounds, a sensation of being trapped. Jann woke to find herself bound to an operating table. Her feet, hands and body were strapped down tight. She turned her attention to her environment and saw that she was in a small room. It was stark, save for some medical equipment of indeterminate function. She lifted her head further to fully examine her situation. It was not good.

The wall in front of her was made from a semi-transparent glass, and she could make out the vague shapes of people moving around on the other side. She struggled against the bonds again, this time with such ferocity that the table shook with her rage. The figures noticed her activity and the glass wall became a little more transparent. She could now see several people sitting at workstations, facing her. One was standing looking straight at her. They all wore white lab coats and odd looking face masks. The standing figure spoke; Jann thought he must be in charge.

"Please, do not be alarmed. We need to restrain you for your own safety."

Jann strained against her bonds again. "Get me out of this."

"If you insist on struggling then we must sedate you again."

Jann stopped. "Who are you? What do you want from me?"

"All in good time, Dr. Malbec."

"How do you know who I am?"

"We know a lot about you. We have been observing you for quite a while."

Jann shook the table again. "Get these off me."

"That is not possible at present. You see, you are a biohazard and as such a contamination risk to us. Please remain calm. You will feel no pain while we conduct our experiments."

Jann fought her bonds with all the strength she could muster, the entire room shook with the violence of her struggle.

"I'm sorry but you leave us no other option." With that, the window dimmed and Jann heard a pump kick in. She looked for the source of the sound and found it was coming from a unit beside her head. From this she could see a clear tube running into her neck, a blue liquid

flowing through it. She slowly felt her muscles relax and all consciousness drain out of her—again.

JANN WOKE with a start and sat bolt upright. Light blinded her and she shaded her eyes to look around. It was the same room but the operating table and the medical equipment were gone. She breathed a sigh of relief when she realized she was no longer restrained. She was lying on a small bed, a pair of soft shoes and a bottle of water on the floor next to her, and nothing else. She stood up, feeling a little shaky, and moved over to the window. It was dull and cloudy, she couldn't make out anything on the other side. She rubbed her wrists, they were bruised and cut where she had tried to free herself from the straps that restrained her. She sat back on the small bed. It was clear to Jann that Colony Two was very much alive and well.

THE SOLS PASSED, one by one. She could tell only by the light in her room dimming at night and growing brighter in the morning. It was a strange light. There was no specific point of origin, it seemed as if the entire upper half of the room glowed with an even luminosity. It had a reddish hue, like the daylight on Mars. At night the light didn't switch off, it simply dimmed slowly over time, like a Martian dusk. But it was never totally dark. At night she could make out the constellations of the nighttime sky. It was like camping out. At one point she reached up and touched the wall, just to check that she was not imagining it. That all this time, she was really outside, as if that were even possible. But she needed some way to anchor her mind to reality. It gave under the touch of her fingers and felt soft, almost velvety. Jann considered that it might be bioengineered. Some sort of phosphorescent living organism that grew across the roof of the room.

Food came to her through a hatch in the wall. The table would first extend then a side panel would open and a tray of food slid onto it. The first time this happened she cowered in a corner on her bed, then sat and looked at it for a while before moving over to check if there was anything she could use as a weapon. There was nothing, no utensils and the dishes were made from some flimsy paper-like material. She picked it up and flung it at the window. But by sol three, she was hungry and sat down to pick at the food. It consisted of salads and some vague, nutty rectangle, presumably protein. She took a tentative sip of water. It tasted fresh and clean, so she drank it all.

Sometimes she could make out vague shapes moving behind the dull window. She would scream and shout at them, bang her fist against it. But it was useless—there was no response.

· · ·

IT WAS EARLY on the forth sol when the door finally opened and in walked a tall, dark, elegant man. Behind him were two others wearing black, one carried a tray of food, the other a long metal bar. They were male, Caucasian, and looked identical.

"Dr. Malbec, you're finally awake. My name is Dr. Ataman Vanji." He extended a hand towards her.

Jann froze for a moment. "The geneticist from Colony One?"

"Ahh, you've heard of me? Yes, one and the same." He shook her hand. "My apologies for the unfortunate nature of your welcome. But we needed to be sure that you were clean."

"Clean?"

"Please, eat." He signaled for the other man to bring forward the tray. He waved a hand over a wall panel and a small table slid out along with a bench on either side. He placed the tray on the table.

"We needed to ensure you were free of the infection. That's why we had to keep you locked up here."

Jann was finding it difficult to formulate any sort of a reply. She stood with her back to the wall, ready to strike at the first opportunity.

"You know about the infection, don't you? Some of your crew succumbed to it."

"Yes," she managed.

Vanji waved a dismissive hand in the air. "It was an error on my part that allowed it to escape into the general environment, before it had been fully developed."

"You can kill it?"

"Oh yes, quite easily really."

"How?"

"As a biologist, Dr. Malbec, I'm sure you are aware of the toxicity of oxygen to certain life forms?"

"Well, yes."

"Expose the bacteria to a low pressure, one hundred percent oxygen environment for twenty-four hours and it is dead. Expose an infected human to the same for thirty-six and they too are free of it. Simple." *Pressure, of course. Why didn't I think of that?* she thought as she slumped down onto the edge of the bed. *How could I have been such an idiot not to have tried that?* Oxygen toxicity was an obvious experiment, and she had tried it several times, but not in combination with a variable pressure environment. All these years, all the hopeless experiments, and now she had her answer. Just like that.

"That's why we needed to keep you sealed in here for a few sols. Come, let me show you what we have done here. I'm sure you have many questions." He stood back and held the door open, inviting her through.

Jann took a moment to compose herself. The shock of what she had just discovered was still reverberating around her mind. Finally she stood up and looked from the door back to Vanji, and then at the two guards standing behind him.

"Come, you have nothing to fear, and as a biologist, I'm sure you'll be fascinated by what we've created."

Jann took a tentative step towards the door. Vanji

had already walked out, leaving the two guards behind. She followed him out into a long, wide corridor hewn from the rock. The walls were rough. Above her, the roof was curved, with the same strange illumination. They walked side by side, the two guards following behind.

"How did you survive? All this time, it must be, what, six years since the sandstorm, since Colony One went offline?"

"We got lucky. Originally we only had solar power, but this whole area beneath our feet," he gestured towards the floor, "has considerable geothermal activity. Aerothermal, to give it its correct terminology, seeing as we are on Mars."

"You mean it's hot?"

"Not exactly hot, but there is a significant temperature difference between the surface and the lower galleries of this cave system. Enough for us to sink deep bores and create a heat exchanger—in fact, several of them. So we were able to generate our own power. That's what saved us. Not only that, it enabled us to create what I'm about to show you."

They came to a stop in front of a metal door set into the rock. Vanji swiped a hand across the control panel and the door opened to reveal a lift. They stepped inside. It was both wide and tall, its interior sleek and well engineered. Jann could feel the lift move a short distance before it came to a soft halt, then seemed to move sideways. Finally the doors opened into a large cave filled with desks, seating and personal items. It looked like Vanji's own private space.

"Please," he gestured towards an armchair. "Have a seat. Are you hungry? I can have some more food brought to you if you like."

"No I'm fine, thanks. Where are we?"

"This is my humble office. It's where I live, really. Let me show you the colony." He moved over to long flat wall and swiped a control panel. Slowly the wall illuminated. Jann thought it was a screen at first. But it was a window, presumably made from the same material as the one in her room. She stood up, moved over to it, and looked out. "Oh my God."

"This is a window into our world. Down there is the soul of Colony Two."

BELOW HER, a vast cavern stretched into the distance. The floor was covered with vegetation and plant life. Here and there she could see small ponds and streams. It was like a lush parkland. Overhead, the cavern ceiling had the same strange illumination. The entire ceiling was light, a diffuse reddish illumination. Strange and incredible, it was like being outside. What startled Jann the most was the population. Throughout the cavern she could see groups of colonists going about their business: planting, harvesting, tending. With just a cursory look, she estimated there must be at least a hundred people down there. How could this be? She turned to Vanji. "All these colonists, where did they come from? There was only supposed to be a few dozen working here when the sandstorm hit."

"Ah, yes. This may come as surprise to you but most of these people are in fact clones. They are my most magnificent achievement: loyal, trustworthy and eternally young." He faced the window and opened his arms wide as if to embrace his creation.

Jann was silent for a while as she tried to comprehend this. So Gizmo was right about clones after all. She should have known, it always was. The colonist that arrived at the airlock at Colony One must have been one of these. But why did he go there? Was he trying to escape?

Vanji turned back to Jann. "I know it's a lot to take in. But give it time and you will begin to understand the society we have created here."

Jann looked up at him. "I'm sure I will, but right now I just want to get back to Colony One as soon as possible."

"Ah... well, you see that's not possible."

Jann stiffened. "What do you mean?"

He looked down and rubbed his chin. "Your arrival here has created something of a dilemma for us. Our existence here is secret and... well, you jeopardize that."

"But how?"

Vanji waved a dismissive hand. "The *how* is not important at the moment. What *is* important is your future here."

"What? I'm not staying here."

"That is not for you to decide. There are those on the Council who demanded you be recycled. But since you're a biologist I think you will make a great addition to our team."

"Recycled? You mean... killed?"

"Not a term we use here. We treasure life; it is a precious resource on Mars. We do not kill, we recycle. You see, our philosophy here is that the soul belongs to the person but their biology belongs to the colony."

"So, what are you saying?"

"I'm saying that this is where you live now, until the time comes for you to be... recycled."

6

BIOLOGY

After her meeting with Vanji, Jann had been taken, under guard, to a different room farther down the long corridor. She was unceremoniously shoved inside and the door locked. The room was like the corridor, hewn from the rock, a cave within a cave. It was spacious, but furnished only with a bed, a desk and a seat. All of which were fabricated from bio-plastic. The ceiling was high and had the now-familiar lighting covering the ceiling. Again she had the disjointed feeling of being outside. She presumed this was now her room for the foreseeable future, however long that future might be.

On the table was a handwritten note. *Place your palm over the touch plate on the desk to activate. To activate what?* she wondered. Inspecting the surface, she found it to be smooth except for a small frosted glass to one side. She placed her palm on it and a 3D image of Mars projected upward and rendered itself just above the desk. *'Welcome Dr. Malbec. Please relax and enjoy this presentation.'* The rendering of Mars grew larger and started to rotate. It zoomed in on the Jezero crater and then on the location of Colony Two.

'In the beginning...' The voiceover commenced. It was a history lesson. Jann sat down and paid attention.

THE MINE WAS FIRST ESTABLISHED by the early colonists, over ten Earth years ago. Initially they open cast for metals and silica but eventually sealed the cave system and created a pressurized atmosphere inside. This single act radically transformed the place and in many respects, as a Martian habitat, it was far superior to Colony One. It had heat from aero-thermal activity deep below the surface. The rock and regolith were free of toxic perchlorates, and the millions of tons of rock above made a perfect radiation shield. No wonder Vanji regarded it as being the perfect crucible in which to forge his vision of humanity. The vast cavern that Jann had witnessed from Vanji's lair was only one of many, a great many. What they had accomplished here was staggering. Not least the incredible advances that they had made in genetic engineering, particularly in human cloning.

YET, the know how to clone a human had already existed, at least in theory. However, it was the ultimate scientific taboo. No scientist in their right mind would touch it. The repercussions of such experimentation would, at best, destroy a career instantly. At worst it would come with a hefty prison sentence. It was banned outright. But of course, that was on Earth, this was Mars. *'The only law on Mars is your own.'* She remembered that first day in Colony One with Paolio, wandering around the biodome. "We've come a long way since then, Paolio," she said to herself.

WHEN THE PRESENTATION FINISHED, Jann sat for a while digesting all that she had gleaned from it. What interested her most was not so much what was said, but what had been left unsaid. Even if Vanji and his team had successfully developed a human clone, it would be a mere baby. All the colonists she saw in the cavern were adults. So how was this possible? And the numbers suggested that there must be more than one clone of the same person. Multiple copies, all created from the same source.

Then there was the secrecy. No one knew this place existed as a functioning colony. Not even Nills. He seemed convinced that no one could have survived the great storm. Or was he also in on it, part of the conspiracy? He had tried hard to hide his own existence from the ISA crew, maybe he knew? But she realized this was not possible. Because what Nills knew, Gizmo would also know, and the little robot had scant data on Colony

Two. She gave a thought to Gizmo, even felt a twinge of sorrow for it, tending to the garden in the vast biodome of Colony One, all alone.

Jann had no answers to any of these questions. So she turned her attention to examining the room. Specifically, how to get out. But after a brief period of testing and prodding she gave up and lay down on the bed. She needed to think.

ON THE PLUS SIDE, she now possessed the knowledge of how to kill the bacteria that had so devastated her life. Oxygen toxicity she knew, and had tried. But not in combination with low pressure. How could she have been so dumb not to have considered it? She could have been home free by now. But there was no point dwelling on it. At least now she knew. It was her passport off this planet, her ticket back to Earth.

Yet even with this, she was further away than when she started. Trapped in a nightmare, with no escape. *There must be a way out*, she thought. At least her mind was beginning to focus now. It was clear to her what her mission was. She would find a way to escape or be *recycled* in the attempt. *What did that mean?* she wondered. Was it death or something halfway in between? Some form of termination that could only be conjured from the mind of a geneticist? It wasn't something she wanted to experience. No, what she wanted was to go home, back to Earth, and be done with Mars and all its insanity.

So, her number one priority would be to find out as much as possible about the inner workings of the colony. Next would be to gain Vanji's trust and to a lesser extent, the trust of the Council. It was clear from her initial discussion with him that they were not all in favor of keeping her alive. Her stay of execution was prompted by Vanji regarding her knowledge as an asset. She needed to play along with this, and in truth, part of her was fascinated to learn all she could about the experiments being conducted here, especially regarding cloning.

In the end, she realized she had little choice but be a part of Colony Two and try not to get herself *recycled*. She remembered Vanji's words. *'The soul belongs to the person but their biology belongs to the colony.'* A shiver ran up her spine.

7

HOMO ARES

Jann awoke to the sound of the door being opened. The light grew brighter and she sat up in bed with a jolt, her body taut, ready for action. The same two black-clad guards entered and took up positions either side of the doorway. They were followed in by a woman carrying a tray of food. Her head was lowered and she moved deftly, but in silence. She put the tray on the desk and retreated, without making eye contact. The two guards followed her out and locked the door again.

Jann relaxed, swung her legs over the side of the bed and stood up. *It must be morning,* she thought. She eyed the tray of food, picked up an apple and took a bite. It tasted good, so she finished it in four bites. She was hungry. Better eat as much as possible as who knows when she would eat again. As someone who had lived the hunter-gatherer lifestyle for the last few years she was not accustomed to eating only when food was available. She cast her eye over the tray again. There were baskets of fruit and bread, a jug of juice and a small platter with what looked like paté. She lifted it up, examined it, sniffed and was pretty sure it was synthetic, probably grown in a lab. Jann put it back and decided the fruit might be the safer option, and chose a pear. She noticed something odd at the bottom of the basket, and reached in to lift it out.

It was a small hard object wrapped in a paper-like material. She opened it to find a note.

'Our joy knows no bounds now that you have come. Your presence amongst us fills us with hope. This token will keep you safe. Tell no one.'

Jann examined the object. It was a small white stone, carved into the shape of the beehive hut near Colony One. Its base was flat and etched on the underside was the word '*Source.*'

She turned it over a few times, examining it. She could tell that it must have been carved some time ago as it was worn and unevenly polished, as if someone had kept it in a pocket. Dirt had accumulated in the word scratched in to the base. It was a strange artifact, its meaning obscure.

She dressed, ate and was back examining the object when the door opened and Vanji strode in. She shoved the object into her pocket before he noticed.

"Ah, Dr. Malbec, are you ready for our little tour? I have something very special to show you today. Come."

Jann stood up and made her way into the corridor, sizing up the two guards. She reckoned she could take them, if she had the element of surprise as an advantage. Relieve one of his cattle prod and the other would go down easy. But she would only get one chance at that, and now was not the time.

They walked to the elevator at the end of the passage and entered. "So where are we going?" asked Jann as Vanji pressed a code into a touchscreen.

"We are going to witness an act of creation in the birthing room." They descended, deep into the bowels of Colony Two. The doors finally opened on a short tunnel, opening out into a wide cavern. The roof had the same, all encompassing lighting. Rows of horizontal glass tanks, each the size of a large bath and filled with a thick, opaque liquid covered the floor. There was something inside but it looked dull and formless through the fluid. Wires and tubes snaked in and around the tanks and they all glowed with a muted luminosity. Vanji led her down a row towards a knot of people gathered around a tank, all busy tending to their tasks. They looked about twenty-five, but Jann doubted that was their actual age.

"Dr. Vanji, we're ready when you are." One technician broke away from the knot and approached them. She eyed Jann with a distinct air of suspicion.

"Excellent." Vanji turned to Jann. "You are now going to witness the birthing of a new life form." He waved his hand at the technician. "You may commence."

The technician retreated with a nod. Activity

increased around the tank as the glow brightened. Jann could now make out the recumbent form of a human. Pumps activated and the level of liquid in the tank slowly decreased. She was close enough to witness the human breach the surface. It was male, fully adult, and also looked around twenty-five. Its entire body was covered in a thin wire mesh, and various tubes snaked from its orifices.

When the last of the fluid drained away, the sides of the tank detached and started to rise upwards into the space above. The technicians gathered around the body, removing tubes and wires in a well-practiced routine, all the time getting feedback on bio-status from monitors. After a few moments they all stood back down. The lead technician turned to Vanji. "He's ready."

"Excellent. You may proceed with the *kick*."

Again the technician nodded, and signaled to the others.

"All clear?" A chorus of confirmations echoed around the platform and the body appeared to be zapped with a high-voltage charge. Its back arched, muscles contracted and it shook, and banged, and vibrated for a few seconds before lying still. Steam rose from the body.

"Again." A technician shouted.

For a second time the body was racked with a high-voltage jolt, longer this time. Finally it stopped and there was a moment of silence. His fingers twitched, his back arched and he took in a long hissing breath. The technicians moved fast, he kicked and shivered and shook as they gathered around him: probing, testing, analyzing. They watched a large monitor: checking stats, verifying data, monitoring readouts. His eyes were wide and frantic, and one of them jabbed his neck with a syringe. He quieted down. They stood back and inspected the monitors.

"Subject's physiological and neural data looks excellent. We can proceed with processing." With that, the technicians started cleaning him before finally lifting him onto a waiting gurney and covering him with a thin sheet. When they were finished they wheeled him off.

JANN STOOD IN MUTE SILENCE, all the while clutching the totem that had arrived with breakfast. She rubbed its smooth face with her thumb; it comforted her. Vanji turned to her as she watched the huddle of technicians wheel the subject out of the birthing chamber. "You have been privileged to witness the creation of life itself. A new colonist to add to our ever-growing population."

Jann was speechless. What could she say that could in any way sum up her emotions? In the end she simply said, "Holy crap."

Vanji threw his head back and laughed. "I fully appreciate your shock at witnessing this event. For the uninitiated it must be a surreal experience."

"So what happens to him now?"

"He will be processed over the next few months until he is ready to join our community."

"Processed?"

"Looks can be deceptive. He may seem fully grown, and in many ways he is, but his mind is like that of a small child. New members require counseling and processing before the full potential of the mind is realized."

"But how can you create a clone so fully formed, so complete?"

"Would you like to see how it's achieved?"

Jann thought about this for a minute. She had just witnessed the creation of a new life, the moment it became cognizant, and that new life was the product of science. Not of nature, per se, but through the genius of one man, Dr. Ataman Vanji. He had stolen the secrets of the gods, the knowledge and ability to create life. Part of her felt that this power was not right, not natural—not moral. But the scientist in her was fascinated. How was this even possible?

"Show me," she said finally.

Vanji stared at her intensely for a moment. Then he smiled and said, "I was right about you, you have the soul of true scientist. That insatiable desire to know and understand. Let me show you."

They walked back along the rows of tanks until they came to a laboratory. Here again, a tank took central position. It was filled with the same opaque viscous fluid but Jann could see it was empty. From around its base ran a myriad of wires and tubes into machines and systems of indeterminate function.

"This is where the magic begins," he indicated the tank. "In here is a biological suspension of stem cells and nutrients. Into this primordial soup we introduce the zygote. It is then stimulated, using a complex radiation process with a specific harmonic frequency modulation. This accelerates the cell division process and as each cell starts to define itself, it gathers to it the raw materials— the stem cells it's surrounded by—and utilizes these to speed up the process of growth."

Jann touched the side of the tank and peered in. "How do you create these stem cells? I mean, there are so many."

"We grow them, and we also recycle."

Jann stepped back from the tank with a jolt. "So that's what you meant. The soul belongs to the human, but their biology belongs to the colony."

"You must understand, this is a barren planet, life is precious here. Nobody should die needlessly. It would be a waste."

Jann put her hand into her pocket and clutched the totem. "Are you creating genetic replicas of all the colonists who came here?"

"Not quite. You see, it is quite a traumatic experience, for an original human to come face to face with their clone. So we have only cloned those that are no longer alive."

"But there must be over a hundred people here."

"Our total population is nearing two hundred."

"So there are multiple clones of the same person?"

"Yes, there are secondary, tertiary and even quad clones. These do not experience the same emotional trauma at meeting their twins. But we are now embarking on a whole new phase. We're creating hybrids."

"Hybrids?"

"Yes, a genetic mix of different colonists. You see, clones are an exact genetic replica of their hosts. But with hybrids, we can introduce biological variation and new genetic enhancements. You see, Jann, we are creating a whole new species of human. We call this new species Homo Ares." Jann shuddered as the implications of Vanji's genetic experiments with the human race began to sink in. "Oh my God." She stepped back from Vanji and stared at him in shock. It took every ounce of her will to keep it together. *Get a grip, old girl, don't let him see,* she thought as she clutched the totem in her pocket tighter.

"Ah, I see you are suitably impressed, as I knew you would be." He had mistaken her body language for admiration, not horror.

Jann looked around at the lab equipment to give herself some time to compose herself. Finally she said, "So tell me, why are there no children? Surely with everyone in the full flush of youth there must have been some pregnancies?"

"Ah, well the clones are sterile and, well... natural reproduction is... forbidden."

"Forbidden?"

"It is too harsh an environment for such fragile biology, and, let's face it, we have a better, safer way of doing it. We think of it as a major evolutionary step for humanity."

"But how do you prevent it? The need to reproduce is the very essence of life."

Dr. Vanji looked down at the floor for a moment. "I wasn't going to mention it right now, but since you brought it up I might as well tell you. All the females have a procedure to make them sterile. And I assure you it is quick and painless, you won't feel a thing."

"What? You're not serious."

"It is not a request, it's for the good of the colony. You must realize this after everything I showed you."

Jann began to feel even more trapped. She looked around anxiously, she wanted to run, to get out now.

"Just think about this," Vanji continued. "When you set foot on this planet for the first time you were in your early thirties. Now, three years later, you have the physical body of a twenty-five year old. This is the gift we have given you. What we ask is a small price to pay for this miracle."

Jann stayed silent and tried to keep from running.

"It is good that you found us, you were using your newfound youth and energy to live like a cavewoman. This was a complete waste of your talents."

"How do you know that?"

"Ah, we may be hidden from the world but there's not much we don't know."

Jann thought about how much had changed. She had gone feral, that much was true, but at least she had freedom, both of thought and action. Yet here, she could possibly be sacrificing her womanhood. In her mind, this was a very high price to pay. She forced herself to stay calm.

"So why all the secrecy, why hide all this from Earth?"

"Just think of what this technology could do to humanity if given free reign. It would destroy them, and possibly the entire ecosystem with it. It needs complete control and we are not ready yet."

Jann had to admit, he had a point. It would do nothing for the human race but sow the seeds of its own destruction. "But, why hide? Why not let them know you're all alive and prospering, but keep silent on the genetic breakthroughs?"

"Because if they know we're here then they will find out. And then they will come and they will simply take it. Do not underestimate the greed of humanity. The lure would be irresistible. So we must wait until the time is right, when we alone can dictate the terms and keep control."

"And when is that?"

Vanji gave her a long look as if considering how much he could reveal. "Soon, the time is very soon. And it is you that has made that possible."

"Me? How come?"

He waved a dismissive hand. "That's enough for today, I think. We can resume our discussion at a later date." He signaled to the ever-present guards. "Please see Dr. Malbec back to her room."

8

THE COUNCIL

Vanji sat at the head of a long table that had been carved from solid rock and polished to a high sheen. On either side sat the members of the colony council. They were all *alphas*, original colonists, and all had a youthful appearance that belied their true ages. No clones, *betas* as they were called, held positions on the ruling council.

He pulled at the cuffs of his robe of office, something he wore only when the council met. It conferred power and status and signified his authority. There was much to discuss, the assembled members were intrigued with rumor and counter-rumor concerning the latest addition to the colony. But, first things first, protocol needed to be observed. Vanji stood and signaled to The Keeper of Records.

"Can we start with the figures for the previous period?" he sat down again.

The Keeper consulted his screen and a 3D rendering of various datasets materialized in the center of the enormous stone table.

"First the good news. We've had a record number of births this period, bringing our total population up to one hundred and ninety three." There was a cursory round of applause at this news. "If we continue at this rate we will reach a population of two hundred in the next period." The Keeper continued, "That said, the rate of discontent and insubordination continues to rise. We recycled three this period, and an increasing number of betas are requiring *correction*." This last set of statistics was met with muted murmurs.

"It seems that our Head of Harmony Sector is failing in her duty to fulfill the requirements of her office. This cannot be allowed to continue." Luka Modric, Head of Operations, pointed an accusatory finger across the table.

"I would challenge that it is our Head of Maintenance that is failing in his duty and is, in fact, the root cause of this discontent. These constant power outages are a cause for concern, not just for betas." Harmony reciprocated by pointing at Maintenance.

"We do what we can with what we have. Some systems are old and spare parts are not easily manufactured here in the colony. Betas still lack the skills to fashion what we need. The population is growing too fast." Maintenance fought back with a resigned acceptance of reality.

"My betas can make anything." Manufacturing

slapped the table. "Anything you asked for, they have made. Have they not?"

"Enough of this bickering, it is not what we need right now." Vanji silenced the council members and then waved at the Keeper to continue with the data report.

The Keeper cleared his throat and continued. "Eh... mining output suffered a sharp drop due to... eh... issues with some of the processing machinery." This was met with silence around the table. "However, we have sufficient supplies in reserve to maintain manufacturing levels in and around those of the previous period."

Manufacturing directed a raised hand at Maintenance. "I rest my case." Manufacturing scowled.

"Food production is 5.6% higher overall, with increases seen in all areas, most notably in that of... eh... wine." This was met with several nods of approval.

The Keeper of Records droned on in this fashion for some time as the ups and downs of colony life were read out in numbers and percentages. When he finally finished the rest of the assembled council breathed a collective sigh of relief.

It was Luka Modric, Head of Operations, who spoke next, as was his right by rank. "So what is the current status of this... ISA crew member?"

"She is being kept under close guard at present while she undergoes a period of psychological readjustment," replied Vanji.

"Is that wise? If word of her existence here gets out, then the betas may become more unsettled. They would find this revelation hard to absorb. If not handled delicately it has the potential to upset the colony." Head of Harmony was concerned.

"It's bad enough that Boateng escaped and made the trip. Now we are living with the consequences of that," said Modric.

"Have we found out how Boateng got access to a functioning EVA suit?" The question was put to Daniel Kayden, Head of Hydro.

"Not yet, but rest assured, we will."

"He had to have help from someone, and it must have been from an alpha," Modric continued.

"Well that makes twenty people, if we include you in that," said Kayden.

"Are you accusing me of having some part in this?"

Kayden raised a hand. "I'm saying you are also an original colonist, as all of us here are."

Vanji leaned into the table. "His trip has proved fortuitous for us. If Boateng had not set out on his quest then the ISA crewmember would not have come to us. She is a biologist of some expertise, so a very useful addition to the colony."

"Yes, but at what cost? What if they have seen it?" Modric pointed skyward. "A satellite may have picked up all this activity."

"All the communication we have intercepted over the past few years indicates that Earth has given up on sending another mission here anytime soon. Even if they have seen something they can't know what it is. It's not going to prompt an invasion." Kayden was hitting his stride.

"Her presence here is a clear danger to the social balance of the colony. The betas already have a strong creation myth developed around Colony One and that beehive hut. That's why Boateng escaped, it's this obsession they have, it grows stronger every sol. Therefore, for the good of the colony, I propose that she be recycled immediately." Modric was adamant.

Vanji raised a hand. "Let's not be so hasty, she could be very valuable to us. And may even help calm the betas."

Modric was having none of this. "I propose a vote, a show of hands. All in favor of recycling the ISA crew member Dr. Jann Malbec?"

A few timid hands were raised. "Well that settles it," said Vanji. "She stays."

BUOYED by this besting of Modric, Vanji considered that now might be a good time to get consensus from the council for his latest creation. He nodded to his Head of Genetics. "Lori, if you will. Now would be a good time to make your presentation."

Lori Bechard tapped some icons on his screen and a 3D rendering of a human rotated above the center of the table. "This is HYB-Q003." He waited a beat to increase the drama. "She will be the first quad-donor hybrid ever created." This was met with interest.

"More hybrids, Vanji? I thought it was agreed by the council that this line of genetic experimentation was to be phased out?"

"It was never *agreed,* Modric. At best it was advisory. The development of hybrid humans is the future, as I've argued many times around this table. We are bringing into being an entirely new race of humans. This is to be celebrated, not denied." Vanji was standing now, one hand on the table, looking directly at Modric. "What's more, the twenty or so hybrids we have in the colony are the best resource we have for keeping the betas from getting ideas beyond their station. In short, Modric, we need them." He slapped the table and sat down.

Lori took this his cue to continue. "HYB-Q003 will be birthed within the next few days and represents a new pinnacle in our genetic cloning program. For the first time, we now have a hybrid clone that is biologically capable of reproduction."

The council erupted.

"What? That is going too far, we cannot allow it." Modric was apoplectic. The others added to his outrage with their own outbursts.

"This is madness."

"Have you lost your mind Vanji?"

"I for one, am not comfortable with this," said Harmony.

"This goes against everything we agreed on."

Modric stood up and raised his hands to quiet them all down. "There is a simple way to settle this once and for all. I propose another vote. A vote to ban all experimentation with hybrid clones, forever. For the good of the colony. All in favor?"

Hands shot up, save for the geneticists and Daniel Kayden.

"Very good." Modric turned to Vanji. "The Council have spoken. There will be no more of this line of experimentation. It is to cease immediately and this... hybrid will be recycled." He sat down.

"You are making a grave mistake." Vanji's face was tight, his body taut, his anger barely contained. "You are throwing away the future evolution of the human race."

"This is not our future, Vanji. Nor will it be. It has been decided. No more of this line of experimentation." Modric waved a dismissive hand.

Vanji seethed. He had been defeated, his ambition thwarted. He had played his hand too soon, grossly miscalculated. He looked around the table at the assembled councilors. They were fools, simpletons with no vision. But now he knew who was on his side.

9

INTRIGUE

Along one section of the upper gallery of the vast main cavern, a common rest and recreation area had been created over time, for alphas only. It was their exclusive domain and no clones could enter, unless of course, they were on the serving staff. It was long, with a low wall running along the edge like a balcony. Above this wall ran a window that afforded those who had sufficient rank to gaze down across the lush vegetation and busy industry of Colony Two. It was one-way, Alphas could see out, but nobody could see in.

When Kayden entered, he noticed that Modric was already there, sitting at one of the far tables facing the window, in a quiet and secluded spot. He played with a drink and looked to be deep in thought. He had asked to meet Kayden here, to discuss things, as he put it. Modric's way of finding out which side he was on, he presumed.

"Modric."

"Kayden, come, sit." He waved a hand at the seat closet to him. Kayden sat. "Drink?" he lifted his glass. "Sol 11,345, an excellent vintage, I would highly recommend it."

Kayden nodded and a glass was poured. Modric raised his own to him. "I would suggest 'to your good health' but that would seem a little self-serving."

"Indeed," replied Kayden, as he took a sip of the fragrant Colony wine. "That was a brave challenge you made, back at the council meeting."

"Perhaps you think it foolhardy? To overrule Vanji like that?"

"The thought had crossed my mind."

"Maybe I grow old. Maybe I tire of this place and this... existence." He looked back at Kayden. "Does it not feel strange to you, that your mind is that of a forty year old but the face staring back at you in the mirror is only twenty-five?"

"Far from it, Modric. I'm constantly amazed at what we have achieved here. Perhaps it's really something else that bothers you?"

Modric looked into his glass for a moment, then looked over his shoulder before leaning in closer to Kayden. "I feel we are living on borrowed time. I sense the betas grow more agitated with each passing sol. It's like we're sitting on a powder keg. Look at us, look around you. We live the exalted life as top dogs in the colony hierarchy. Yet we are few. Every time Genetics births a new beta we become more of a minority. And the history of societies ruled by minority elites never ends well."

"Ha, you're being paranoid." Kayden laughed and quaffed his wine, refilling his glass from the bottle on the table between them.

"Maybe. But you know this creation myth that the betas have developed around Colony One is getting very strong."

"Yes, I've heard rumors. Is it really true?"

"It gets more ingrained with them every sol." He sat back. "It's because of their dreams. Strange, don't you think, that they should all have the memories of the alpha they were cloned from? Growing more lucid as they age."

"Yes, but that's what makes them so useful. Without these dreams they would know nothing, they would have to learn like children. It would take years before they are productive."

"Well it's a double edged sword, one I hope we don't all fall on."

They stayed silent for a moment and gazed down across the vast cavern. Betas were working away, planting, harvesting and maintaining the lush garden.

"It's the reason Boateng escaped and tried to journey to Colony One. It's this... desire that is awakening within them. It grows stronger and stronger."

GERALD M. KILBY

Kayden considered this, but stayed silent. Modric continued, "Look, it was bad enough that he got out. But now, the last ISA crewmember shows up at our door." He pointed skyward. "They must have seen all this activity. Earth must suspect something by now, assuming they still have a working satellite up in orbit. We cannot remain hidden much longer."

"I'll grant you that, Modric. This is a concern."

"We are entering uncertain times. This ISA woman is nothing but bad news. Why did Vanji allow it?"

"I don't know. He sees something in her. She's a biologist, apparently."

"Her presence only serves to undermine the harmony we have maintained with the betas. She's from Colony One, to them she is a God, don't you see?"

They went quiet again. Each sipping wine, each deep in thought. After a few moments Modric refilled their glasses and sat forward.

"We have all toiled under the shared belief that we cannot let Earth have this technology: genetic manipulation, longevity, the ability to clone humans. The population would explode and ultimately destroy what's left of the planet."

"If they find out we're here they will come. They will simply take it; we are still not strong enough to stop them. You know this, Modric."

"If we are not strong enough now, then when? Do we need a population of three hundred, or five hundred, or what?" There is no clear plan that I can see. Meanwhile

70

we can't venture out, we can't utilize the resources that we know exist in Colony One, nor can we receive supplies from Earth, even trade with them. In the meantime, we are fracturing. There are essential parts we simply cannot manufacture here. What happens when one of these fails, we all die? What good is the secret of eternal youth if we're dead?"

"You're being overly dramatic. We have power, heat, water and food a plenty."

"A society needs more than that to keep harmony, you know that as well as I do."

"We live in dangerous times, make no mistake."

"Indeed."

Modric looked around to check if they were alone and leaned in again. "Here's what I propose. We kill her. Before she has a chance to infect the minds of the betas. Do it now, while her presence here is still under wraps."

Kayden looked at Modric and took another sip from his glass as a way of giving himself time to think before replying. He placed the glass back down the table with a slow precise movement. "How do you propose we do this?"

"That, I don't know. I thought you might be able to offer a possible course of action. Seeing as Vanji looks to you as an ally. You would be least suspected."

"No one could know of this, or we'll be the ones being recycled."

"I fear if we don't, then our days here as leaders are numbered."

Kayden stood up and leaned in to put a hand on Modric's shoulder as he spoke. "Let me sleep on it. That's all I can do for now."

"Don't sleep too long, or we may miss our opportunity."

10

HYDRO

In the sols following Jann's experience in the birthing rooms, she gained a little more freedom, or at least the sense of it. This was limited to short sessions in the bio-labs with the genetics team. She met few colonists save for Vanji, the two guards, and the woman who brought her food. Yet she learned a lot, not just about the complexities of human cloning but also the social hierarchy of the colony. The technology underlying this human outpost might be at the pinnacle of human achievement, but the social structure was medieval.

Alphas ruled. The twenty or so original colonists who had survived all that Mars had thrown at them formed the bulk of the council. They controlled everything. The workers were the betas, the clones. They were created from the *seeds*, as they were known. These turned out to be the Analogues that Jann and the original ISA crew had found in Colony One. No alpha living in Colony Two had been cloned, so the betas were the reincarnation of all those who had died. And there were multiples of each. So far Jann had only met one, the woman who brought food to her room. She was Caucasian, young, and carried herself with a submissive deference, reminding Jann more of the polite manners of a Geisha, never looking her directly in the eye.

But like any technology, it never stood still and Vanji and his team had progressed to creating hybrids. This was more than just cloning, this was human genetic engineering taken to a whole new level. They had effectively created a new species, Homo Ares, Ares being the Greek god of Mars. The two guards were hybrids. Tall, strong, elegant—and silent. They never spoke, but Jann began to notice that, at times, they would look intently at each other, as if they were communicating. They would subtly nod or shake their heads along with almost imperceptible facial twitches. It was eerie to witness, and not a little unsettling.

At the top of this hierarchy was the imperial master, Vanji. He was like an Emperor, feared and worshiped in equal measure. He bestowed the gift of life and possessed the power to take it away with nothing more than a simple edict, a click of his fingers, so to speak. Most of the alphas feared Vanji and the betas feared the alphas. As for the hybrids, they seemed to be oblivious to everything. At least, that's how Jann perceived it.

After a few more sols of obedience they rewarded her

with a window. Still confined to her room save for the odd excursion to the bio-labs, it was a blessing. It was something to break the boredom, and the increasing feeling of being trapped that was fermenting inside her. She had taken to pacing the room, bisecting it in a steady rhythm like the caged animal that she was. It was during one of these pacing sessions that the long smooth wall behind the desk became transparent. She stopped her pacing, crept forward and looked out. The entire vista of the main cavern was laid out below her, vast, verdant and industrious. She spent many hours just observing, following the patterns and rituals of the betas that toiled there. But in the end, all this anthropological study brought her no closer to escape. In fact, she feared she would somehow grow complacent, more accepting, and lose her desire for freedom, maybe even her will to live.

Eventually, on or around the tenth sol of her captivity, a new face entered her room. It was Daniel Kayden, one of the councilors. Behind him stood the same two guards. He smiled as he entered and reached to shake her hand. "Some good news for you, Dr. Malbec. We are paying a visit to a very special place this sol."

"Good, let's go, this room is making me demented. When am I getting out of here?"

"I don't know, that hasn't been decided yet."

"Why the hell not?"

"Look, please be patient, it's just politics." He opened his hands and shrugged his shoulders. "Come, follow me, we can talk as we walk."

Jann quelled her frustration. At least she was getting out for a while, why jeopardize it? They walked side by side in silence, the two guards following in step behind. Jann glanced back at them, their faces were a complete blank.

"Are they hybrids?" she jerked a thumb over her shoulder.

"Yes."

"They don't say much, do they?"

"No, none of them do."

"Are they engineered that way?"

"I'm sorry, I don't know. I'm not one of the geneticists."

"So, what's your story then?"

"I'm a geologist, Head of the Hydro sector."

"Water?"

"Yes, H2O, and I'm taking you to see some."

"Water?"

"Ah," he smiled. "Yes, water, but not like anything you've seen before."

They stepped into the elevator and descended. It felt to Jann that they were going lower than before, lower than the bio-labs. It was also getting noticeably warmer.

The doors opened into a short corridor that led into a pumping station. The sound of engines reverberated around the room. It was loud and mechanical. Large industrial pipes and ducts crisscrossed the space. At the far end was a control board with three betas monitoring the systems. At least Jann assumed they were betas.

"It's very warm in here."

"Yes, we are deep down, close to the aero-thermal engines. It gets even hotter the farther down you go."

"Well I hate to break it to you, but this is not very interesting."

Kayden turned to her and smiled. "Ah, just wait, you'll see."

As they moved past the control station, the three betas straightened and turned to her. She could have been mistaken but it looked to her like they all bowed.

"Are they doing that for you or me?"

"Both. But they do seem fascinated by you. It's the first time they've seen an outsider. You're something of a celebrity to them."

Jann looked back, they were just standing there staring at her as she passed. She nodded at them. This action resulted in their looking amazed and they bowed even lower.

"Come, just ignore them, this way."

They continued on through a short tunnel lined with pipes that finally opened out into a large cave. The floor was sandy and the roof bright, but in the middle was something Jann never thought she would see on Mars. It was a large lake of flowing water.

"Wow."

"Told you."

"This is incredible."

The sandy floor of the cavern extended out to meet the water, like a beach. The lake itself seemed to disappear into a cloud of mist off in the distance. The cavern roof was peppered with long stalactites, and she could hear the water dripping down from their tips.

"The aero-thermal activity is more intense the farther in you go." Kayden pointed towards the back of the cavern. "That's what creates the mist. It's colder overhead so the moisture condenses and drips down, creating these huge stalactites."

"Like rain."

"Yes, like rain. On Mars."

At the edge of the sandy beach a small jetty with a floating pontoon tethered to the end extended into the lake. All along the water's edge seating had been set up.

"Is this where you go for a vacation?"

Kayden laughed. "Yeah, you could say that. Come, let's get onboard the pontoon and we can see the cavern from the middle of the lake."

They walked across to the jetty and Kayden held his hand out for Jann as she stepped onto the pontoon. It was flat and square with a low handrail on all sides. They hunkered down and Kayden picked up a paddle. "Here, you grab this, I'll cast off."

Jann moved closer to the center of the pontoon, where it felt more stable.

Two guards stood stiff and silent, watching. They became slightly more animated when Jann and Kayden cast off.

"It's okay, we'll only be a short while." Kayden shouted over to them. They relaxed.

"What's with them?"

"Just paddle. We'll take it out to the middle."

They moved with a graceful silence, the only sounds were the paddles hitting the water and the drip-drip from the cavern roof.

"Have you found any life in here?"

"You mean any microbial Martians swimming around?"

"Yes. It would seem ideal, water, heat and lots of complex chemical compounds."

"Sorry to disappoint, but no, nothing."

Jann looked back to see how far they had come. They had skirted the edge of the lake, around a rocky outcrop, and were now out of sight of the guards. They slowly paddled out from the edge, towards the middle of the steamy lake. Then a thought struck Jann. She knew next to nothing about Kayden, or his intentions.

She looked down into the water. "Is this toxic?"

"Yeah, but don't worry, it won't kill you if you fall in, as long as you get out quickly. That said, you could still drown in there. Hell of a way to go, drowning on Mars."

Jann withdrew her paddle. "If it's okay with you, let's head back, I've seen enough."

"Just a bit more, keep paddling."

She reluctantly resumed, but kept a tight grip on the paddle—in case she needed it as a weapon.

MIST BEGAN to envelop them before Kayden finally

reversed his stroke. The pontoon came to a halt. "Okay, I think this should be far enough."

"Those guards back there," he nodded in the direction of the beach. "Are Vanji's eyes and ears. And what I have to say to you is not for them to hear. That's why I took the precaution of bringing you out here." Jann gripped her paddle.

"We don't have much time, so I'll be quick. Here it is. We have a plan to help you escape."

Jann was not sure if this was a trick or some test of Vanji's.

"Escape?"

"It may come as a surprise to you, but some of us don't like what's going on here. We want out, and that's where you come in. How would you like to get back to Earth?"

"Are you serious?"

"Yes."

Jann paused for a moment. "Go on... I'm listening."

"We know that the Odyssey transit craft is still in orbit, still functioning. And that the MAV is intact, it can still be used."

"It has no fuel tanks, they were all destroyed."

"We know the ISA sent you information on how to manufacture them. So we have everything we need to escape, am I right?"

Jann wondered how much Kayden really knew. "In theory, yes. They've been fabricated, but they still need to be filled, checked and transported."

"How long would that take?"

Jann shrugged. "I don't know, at least a sol."

Kayden considered this, as if he were recalculating his escape plan based on this new information from Jann. He stayed silent, thinking.

Jann interrupted his thoughts. "How do you propose we get out of here? Just sneak out at night? I don't think we'd get very far."

"Look, it can be done." Kayden seemed irritated. "But we need *you*, as you are the only one who knows the launch sequence."

Jann thought about this for a moment. Escaping undetected might be possible—with the right help. And Kayden certainly fit that bill. After all, Boateng had done it. But what Kayden was suggesting regarding the MAV was reckless. They would first need to get back to Colony One, then transport fuel tanks back to the MAV, connect them, check all systems and then *hope* that it all worked when the button was pressed. It was insane. There was no guarantee that the MAV would not simply blow up with them inside. Considering it had sat there for three years it would need time to do all the proper preliminary checks. Furthermore, there was also a time issue in coordinating with the Odyssey orbiter, it all needed to be carefully set up. Perhaps Kayden didn't fully understand this.

On the other hand, Kayden was offering her a way out of here. As for getting off the planet, well... she could just play along with that—for the moment.

He looked over at the edge of the lake. "We can't stay here too long, the hybrids will be twitching. Are you in?"

"Okay, where do I sign?"

"Excellent." He clapped his hands together. "Let's head back. We'll find another opportunity to talk more."

They returned to the jetty. The guards had not moved. But Kayden was right, they were twitching a lot more than usual. They stood face to face, looking directly at each other, seemingly not noticing Jann and Kayden stepping off the raft and onto the jetty. "What are they doing?" Jann whispered.

"I honestly don't know. They all started doing this weird staring match with each other a few months back. Strange isn't it?"

"Has anyone *asked* them what they're doing?"

"They say they're just passing the time."

"Really?"

"You don't need to concern yourself with it. Best to just ignore them."

THEY MADE their way back to the upper galleries and Jann was escorted to her room. No more was spoken of the plan. She assumed they would meet again under some other pretext and the details would be outlined. In the meantime all she could do was wait. She sat on the small seat and looked out over the main colony. She felt her pocket for the object she had been given. It was gone. "Crap, where is it?"

She searched the room frantically, around the floor, on the desk, and through the pockets of the few clothes she had been given. It was gone, along with the note. "Damn, they must have found it."

She thought that possibly the beta who brought her food might get into trouble for it. Jann felt she had let her down, she should have taken better care of it. *Too late now*, she thought.

She sat in silence for a while, and watched the to-and-fro of the betas working all across the cavern floor. They moved in random patterns, in and out through the vegetation, planting, harvesting, tending. It had a hypnotic rhythm and Jann felt the stress being gently expelled from her body. Maybe now that Kayden had given her hope she could *stand down*, so to speak. She moved her gaze away from the betas and started to observe the hybrids. Before encountering the strange behavior today at the lakeside, she had not given them much thought, save for how she could take one down. Now though, she began to notice them, pick them out from the other colonists. From what she could see they made up around ten percent of the colony's population. They seemed to do nothing except monitor the betas, always silent, always watchful. But every now and then two or three would group together and do that same weird face to face communicating, their facial muscles twitching. Anytime this happened the betas would distance themselves. It was bizarre.

What was Vanji really creating? They were human,

that much was true. But they clearly displayed traits incompatible with human behavior. They were a different species, a step up on the evolutionary tree. It was how a Neanderthal might have felt observing Homo sapiens communicating. They were the same—but different.

Then something extraordinary happened. The betas had all congregated in one area, just below her, and in unison, they all looked up—directly at her. Just for a moment, then they dispersed.

She jumped up. "Holy shit, can they see me?" It happened so fast that she wasn't sure it really occurred. Maybe she was hallucinating? Jann gripped the back of the chair to steady herself. "What the hell was that?" She retreated to her bed and curled up. She could take no more of this place. She just had to get out. The sooner the better.

11

RECYCLING

J ann tossed and turned, her sleep was fitful. She awoke to the shadow of a beta moving in the room. It was morning and they had come to bring her food, but it was not May, the woman that had come before, it was someone different. Jann sat up and rubbed the sleep from her eyes. "Where's May?"

The beta kept his head down and did not look directly at her. "She has been... eh, reassigned. Please eat. You will be required at the council meeting shortly." He turned and walked out. *Council meeting?* she wondered. Finally she was going to meet the rest of the original colonists. *Should be interesting.*

Jann got up and sat at the desk, eating and looking out across the main colony. She watched the betas going about their business, half expecting to witness a repeat of the previous evening's occurrence. But there seemed to be a different dynamic going on. She couldn't put her finger on it, but a different mood prevailed.

The door finally opened and the two guards stepped in. One spoke, "Come with us, please." It was the first time she had ever heard them speak. It was deep and sonorous, and had a mellow soothing quality to it. Jann was so surprised that all she could do by way of a reply was stare wide-eyed and nod. They all moved down the long corridor, one in front of her, one behind, to a doorway near to where Vanji had first shown her the colony. They entered unannounced. Along both sides of a long stone table sat the Council. At its head was Vanji. Behind him was a glass wall with doors opening out onto a terrace. She could see the cavern roof in the background.

"Ah, Dr. Malbec, please be seated." Vanji pointed at a vacant seat at the far end of the long table.

The two guards took up position either side of her. Jann scanned the council members. They all wore similar off-white clothing. But each had a different color patch sewn on the breast. Vanji, however, wore a purple robe of some kind, perhaps as an indication of his rank and power. She noticed many of the council wore a patch of the same color. Jan wondered if these were the geneticists, presumably the highest ranked citizens of the Colony Two social hierarchy. They sat close to Vanji. She also spotted Kayden. He was closer to her and had a blue patch on his tunic. He didn't make eye contact with her.

"I have something to show you," Vanji began. From a

pocket he took out the object that Jann had been given by the beta on that first sol. He carefully set it on the table. "We found this in your room. We would like to know how you came by it."

"It was in the fruit basket." There was no point in trying to hide it, Jann reckoned they knew already. But her response set off a ripple of murmurs around the table. Vanji raised a hand to silence them.

"Do you know what it is?"

"I'm guessing it's a replica of the beehive hut, out past the dunes near Colony One."

"You are correct. But it is also evidence of something we have begun to suspect."

"Which is?"

"Which is the existence of a creation myth amongst the betas." This brought more animated murmuring from the council members.

"This must be stamped out!" One member slapped the table. "We can not allow this to gain traction."

Vanji raised a hand and turned back to Jann. "You see, betas retain fragments of the memories of their alpha when they are birthed. Why? We are not sure. But that is irrelevant, the fact is they do. Now, this is very useful as they can be conditioned much faster and trained to utilize the technical know-how of their forbearer. But they also have memories, dreams, that become more lucid over time and these memories can drive them to seek out the past. It became a creation myth and it has the potential to undermine everything we are doing here."

"That's a bummer," said Jann.

"You may scoff, Dr. Malbec, but this concerns you, more that you think."

"How so?"

"Because rumor has it that they have a clandestine leader. One that unites them. Some say it's a deity, a god, if you will. If this *leader* were to become strong... well, let's just say the harmony of the colony would be in jeopardy."

"So what's that got to do with me?"

He picked up the object from the table, examined it for a moment, and put it back down slowly.

"We believe that you are this deity they worship."

Jann laughed. "Maybe I should be honored."

That sent the council apoplectic. "Quiet!" Vanji shouted above the clamor. They quieted down. Jann sensed an ugly mood developing.

"You need to understand that these *dreams* are of the past, of Colony One. They are becoming obsessed with it. They seek it, like a Mecca. It will drive them crazy. And you represent that to them. A visitor from Colony One is like a god descending on the multitude."

Jann was silent this time.

"She needs to be recycled."

"Yes, this situation is too dangerous."

"It has to be done."

"We should never have let her in here in the first place."

The table was erupting around her, they wanted her head on a plate.

Vanji raised a hand again and they settled down. "Kayden, what is your opinion? You have been very quiet so far."

Jann looked at the Head of Hydro, her fate totally in his hands. It seemed like an age ago when he had given her hope, a way to escape; now everything had changed.

Kayden looked down and fumbled with the sleeve of his garment. "In the light of these revelations, it would seem the only option is recycling."

"What!" She had been betrayed. She jumped up and her arm was grabbed by one of the guards. But Jann twisted fast and buried two knuckles into the guard's throat. He dropped; she knew she could take them down. She bolted out the door and into the corridor, but she didn't get far. She felt a sting in her neck and touched a small needle. She pulled it out and threw it on the floor. But it had done its job. Her head felt heavy and she quickly lost all control of her body. She collapsed on the floor, face down, Her eyes closed and she lost consciousness.

12

THE TANK

In the time after conception, cells divide and multiply, growing exponentially more numerous. It is from this clump of living matter that all of which defines our biological makeup stems. Hence the term *stem cells*. They possess within them the power to become anything and everything. The genius of Vanji was not the ability to choose what was created, humanity already possessed this knowledge. Nor was it the ability to speed up this process, although that too was a major breakthrough. No, it was the ability to reverse engineer.

How to take a clump of stem cells and turn them into an organ was known. But to take an organ and turn it into stem cells was knowledge of a totally different order of magnitude. This was the genetic alchemy that he controlled. This ability to biologically *recycle*.

It was Jann's fate that soon, she too would experience this biological transformation. Like a zygote in the womb that needs nourishment and sustenance to grow and develop, so too does the body that is to be recycled. That is why subjects were submerged in the bio-tanks alive. And they were kept that way until the point at which they were biologically incapable of consciousness. But unlike a human that takes nine months to be fully viable, the reverse process was much quicker—it only took a month.

JANN SLOWLY BECAME aware of conscious thought, like awakening from a dream. But she existed only in her mind, and so began to focus and tentatively assess the extent of her physical existence. There was none.

She felt a wave of panic rise up from deep within her core. She had no physical sensation, no sight, no sound, nothing to define the limits of her body. She was pure thought, nothing more. *Jesus, what have they done to me?* Fear graduated to terror. She knew what was happening, she was slowly being biologically dissolved. How was this to end? How long would she be conscious of this horror? Hours, sols, weeks?

Time ceased to have meaning. Her thoughts could have occupied a few seconds or an eternity, she had no way of knowing. She felt like she was floating out in the vacuum of space, except there were no stars to orient her. She simply existed in nothingness. There was no pain, at least that was something. But to endure like this, knowing what was happening to her, was a slow descent into a tortured insanity. In the end, there is no more terrifying a place than your own mind.

A VIBRATION. Was she dreaming? No, she felt it again, slight, but it was there, all around her. How could she feel it? She probed the extremities of her body and began to sense her physical being. It grew in intensity and she forced herself to move some part of her. With every fiber of her being she bent her will to the task, to lift a finger, to open an eye, anything. Then the dam burst and she was released from her viscous sarcophagus in a deluge. She broke through to the other side. Voices. She could hear voices, distant, indistinct. Vague lights swam across her vision and she felt her throat being ripped from the inside. It was the tube being pulled out. She gasped and spat and retched. Her body temperature plummeted and pain bound itself to every nerve. Voices. More voices.

"SHIT, SHE'S GETTING HYPOTHERMIA."

"I told you we should have done it in stages. This could kill her."

"We don't have time, quick get her into the blanket, switch it on, get her warm. Shit, don't let her have a cardiac arrest."

"Christ, she's no good to us like this."

"It will pass, trust me, she's been in the tank for less than an hour. Just keep her warm."

"How the hell are we going to get her into an EVA suit like this?"

Jann felt something warm wrap itself around her, and an oxygen mask was held over her mouth. Her shaking began to subside.

"She's okay."

"Thank god for that."

"Right, let's get moving. We only have a twenty-five minute window and we've already used seven."

JANN STILL SHOOK AND SHIVERED, but less with each passing minute. She tried to open her eyes and speak. "It's okay, we got you out." Someone placed a hand on her head; she went quiet again. She could feel herself being carried on a stretcher of some kind. It was dim but she began to make out lights here and there as they moved. After a while they stopped and set her down. She was beginning to come around and tried to lift a hand to wipe her forehead but she felt pinned down, and her mouth was like sandpaper. "Water," she croaked. "Some water?"

"She's coming out of it," someone said.

"Water."

"Wait, hold on, let me get you out of this thermal blanket." Jann could feel the heat drain away as the blanket deflated. She could move again. Someone unzipped it a little and placed a bottle of water against her lips. She raised a hand to hold it as she lifted herself up on her elbow. She drank it all.

GERALD M. KILBY

"Feeling better?" Kayden knelt down beside and took the empty bottle.

Jann sat up and ran her fingers across her face and over her skull. She shook her head and looked at Kayden. "Bastard, you put me in there."

"The Council put you in there. I had no choice but to go along with it, otherwise they would have suspected me. Anyway, you're out now. Time to leave."

"Jesus, I thought I was going to go insane in that tank."

"Think you can stand? We don't have much time." Kayden put a hand under her shoulder." Samir, give me some help here."

Together they lifted her into a standing position. She was shaky, but her body was beginning to recalibrate itself back to normality. She was still wet with slime from the tank. She shivered in horror when she realized, and started to frantically wipe herself down with the blanket that was still partly wrapped around her. "Get this crap off me."

"It's okay, Jann. Just calm down, it's inactive outside of the tank. Just take a deep breath."

She clutched the blanket close to her as the panic began to subside. She let out a deep breath. "Okay, I'm okay." She looked around. They were in a small, dimly lit storeroom. "Where is this place?"

"Near the main entrance to Colony Two."

There were two others with Kayden. Samir, who was

speaking to her now, and another woman who looked agitated.

"I don't suppose you have some clothes for me? Or do I go around naked?"

"The best sort, we've got your EVA suit. Think you can handle it?"

"If it means getting out of this place, then, yeah, lead me to it."

"Behind here." Samir started moving storage boxes out of the way.

"Noome, get Jann some more water. I'll help Samir with the suits." Kayden started to move more of the storage boxes.

Hidden in behind them were four EVA suits. Samir started to check them one by one. "Looking good. Fully prepped, should do the job."

"I hope you're right, they all look a bit ragged, save for Dr. Malbec's." Noome was giving Jann a second bottle of water.

"They may look like shit, but they'll get the job done."

"Come on, we're wasting time." Kayden started to get into his suit.

"Shhhh..."

"What?" whispered Noome.

Samir placed a finger over his mouth. "Listen."

They all stopped and looked towards the door. Footsteps—getting closer.

"Shit."

"Shhhh."

The sound of footsteps stopped outside. Jann looked around for a weapon to arm herself with as they all waited for the door to open. A moment passed, then another, and another, but the door stayed closed. Voices, hybrids—even Jann could recognize their deep resonant tone. Then the sound of movement, more footsteps, this time heading away from the door, back down the corridor, disappearing into silence.

"Whoa, what was that? Noome was trembling with fear, clutching Samir's arm. He wasn't much better.

"Hybrids. Looks like we had a close encounter," said Kayden.

"That was weird, why didn't they come in? They must have known someone was in here."

"Who knows, who cares. They didn't, that's all that matters. Come on let's get going before they come back."

It took them all a few minutes to get suited up and checked. The plan, as far as Jann understood it, was to enter the main Colony Two airlock. This was where they had stashed her rover. They would commandeer it, open the main airlock door and head for Colony One. As an escape plan, she didn't like it, way too risky, too high a chance of being spotted or setting off some alarm when the main airlock door opened. They had nearly been rumbled once so far, and they might not be so lucky again. But there was no other way of getting to Colony One. They had to risk it.

Kayden slowly opened the door and peered out,

looking up and down the corridor. "All clear, let's go." He stepped out and waved to the others to follow. They all had the heavy suits on but carried their helmets, they wouldn't need them just yet. They tried to move quietly but it was difficult. It took them a few minutes to pass through into the main entrance cavern for Colony Two. It was dark but as Samir and Kayden swept the area with a flashlight Jann could see it housed not just one but two pressurized rovers along with a myriad of other small vehicles.

"Samir, go open the inner door. We'll get the rover started." Kayden pointed off to one side of the cavern. The rest of them clambered into the rover and Jann started it up just as the inner door opened. Samir ran back and hopped in. She ran through systems checks to ensure pressure and then drove into the airlock. The door automatically closed behind them and there was a moment or two of nervous waiting before the outer door opened. It was pitch black outside as Jann slowly inched the machine out onto the Martian surface.

IT WAS slow progress at first, and the lights on the rover had little range. But her confidence grew, and the farther they got from Colony Two, the faster she pushed it. There was a collective mood of relief. "We did it, we did it." Noome was ecstatic and slapped Samir on the back. He ventured a smile in return.

Jann pushed the machine as fast as she dared in the

darkness. "I saw a bunch of other rovers in that cavern. Did anyone think to disable them?"

"Don't worry, they haven't moved in years. This is the only operational one," said Kayden.

"I hope so, because it's going to take time to get the tanks ready. We don't want them following us." Jann started to slow down a bit.

"Once we get to Colony One, we're home free. They can't get there, not for a while anyway."

"How can you be so sure?"

"Trust me, we have a sol or two head start, that should be enough time."

Jann felt relief ripple through her. She pushed the rover as hard as she dared to get more distance between her and the nightmare of Colony Two. She was running away, yet again. She felt like she had spent a lot of her time on Mars running away from one thing or another. Someday, she would have to stop.

13

COLONY ONE

They had been moving slowly across the Jezero crater for over an hour, Jann reckoned. Assuming Kayden was right and the other vehicles in the cavern were out of commission, they were in no immediate danger of being followed. So she decided to drive with caution. The last thing she wanted now was to run into a gully or get caught up in a sand dune. Nonetheless, they were making progress and getting close to Colony One. The mood in the rover was one of fatigue mixed with excited relief.

"THERE IT IS, OVER THERE, LOOK." Jann pointed out into the darkness at the lights on the roof of the Colony One biodome. Noome and Samir got up from their seats in the back and leaned into the cockpit to get a better look.

"Cool," said Noome. "I had nearly forgotten what it was like, it seems like so long ago since we left there. Wish I never did."

"Yeah, it doesn't seem so bad after all this time."

During the journey Jann discovered that it was these two that had been tracking the Odyssey craft and intercepting ISA communications. They were original colonists but not on the council, they wanted no part of Vanji's vision of Colony Two. How they hooked up with Kayden, Jann had not yet found out. Not that she cared, she was free of the place and now had a way off Mars, and a return ticket to Earth.

They stood there for a while just watching the lights getting closer until eventually Jann reached down and tapped a few icons on the comms panel.

"Gizmo, this is Jann Malbec, are you still there, over?"

"Gizmo? Who's Gizmo? I thought you were alone in there?" said Kayden.

"I was the only human."

"So who's Gizmo?"

"You'll see soon enough—I hope."

"Gizmo, are you receiving this, over?" Her call was met with static coming over the rover comm as she waited for a reply. Finally, it crackled into life.

"Dr. Malbec, this is a surprise. Do you realize I calculated the probability of your existence being compatible with life at 0.03%?"

"Nice to know you still care, Gizmo."

"*I have been tracking a rover crossing the crater for some time now, I assume this is you?*"

"It is. I have three other people with me, we're heading for the workshop, can you ensure it's got atmosphere?"

"*Certainly, Jann. I am here to assist.*"

"Okay, we'll be there shortly, we can catch up when we arrive. Over and out."

"Who was that?"

Jann looked over and smiled. "Like I said, that's Gizmo, and you'll meet very soon."

SHE PULLED up outside the main workshop airlock with a jolt. Dust and sand rose up all around as the wheels skidded to a halt. Through the swirling dust they could see the door beginning to rise as a crack of light pushed back the night. They drove in, pressurized and finally came to a stop inside the workshop. Jann got out of the rover first, followed by the others.

Gizmo raced over to her and waved a metal hand. "Welcome back, Jann."

"Thank you, Gizmo."

"At the risk of sounding sentimental, I was beginning to miss your company."

Jann gave the little robot a smile. "Me too, Gizmo." She turned to the others. "Kayden, Noome, Samir, meet Gizmo."

The little robot raised a hand. "Greetings Earthlings."

"Wow, that's a pretty cool droid," said Noome. "Where did it come from? I don't remember there being a robot here."

"The last colonist here built it. Nills Langthorp."

"Nills?" said Kayden. "Well, I'm not surprised. He's an amazing engineer, if his clone is anything to go by."

"Nills has a clone?" Jann stopped and looked at him.

"Yeah, of course. There were two of him, I believe, but one got recycled for some reason, I can't remember."

"Inciting insurrection," said Samir.

"Nills-beta is one of the main engineers in Colony Two. I don't think the place would function without him. I think that's why he gets away with so much." Kayden continued.

"With what?"

"He's a leader amongst the betas, if you're to believe the Colony Two rumor mill. He's well respected, and not someone that can be gotten rid of without very good reason. He's too valuable a resource and he keeps the betas in line," said Samir.

"Nills is alive?" said Gizmo.

"Yes and no, his clone is."

"I would very much like to meet him again."

"Me too," said Jann. "But I don't think that's going to happen as we are leaving this planet as soon as possible."

"Leaving?" replied the little robot.

"Yes, on the MAV, so we need to get the new fuel tanks organized. What's the status on them?"

"Fabrication was complete some time ago, but they need to be filled with fuel, and then a diagnostics run to check integrity."

"How long?"

"Best estimate, thirty-six point seven hours."

"What? We don't have that much time," said Noome. "They'll find us before then."

"Thirty-six hours?" Kayden directed his question to Gizmo.

"Approximately."

"Shit, shit." Noome started jumping around. "This is not good, not good."

"Kayden, you better get a handle on her or I will kill her myself."

"Noome, we still have enough time, they won't find us that quick." Kayden's voice was measured.

"How can you be so sure? You're just talking shit."

Kayden grabbed her by the arm. "Listen, just put a sock in it. This isn't helping us."

Noome settled down—a bit.

Jann turned around to face them. "Okay, it is what it is, so here's what we're going to do. We need to get into the main Colony One facility. That means EVA, there's no way through from here. The propellant processing plant is in dome five. Gizmo can run through the procedures once we're inside. It's going to take a while so if they come for us before we're ready then we can defend ourselves better in there. Also I need to clean up, I feel like shit. Anyone got any problems with that, Noome?"

They all shook their heads, even Noome.

"Sounds good to me," said Kayden.

They started to get their suits ready to EVA. Kayden approached Jann. "I was just thinking, seeing as how you're the only one who knows the launch sequence for the MAV, maybe it would be a good idea to tell me, just in case anything happens to you. You know, otherwise we could all end up stranded."

Jann looked back at the renegade council member. "Well then, you better make sure nothing happens to me."

"Yeah, but..."

"Ready to go?" Jann snapped her helmet on.

THEY MADE their way out of the workshop and along the outside perimeter of the Colony One facility. Gizmo raced ahead and got the main airlock ready. As they walked, Jann noticed that Samir and Noome would look out across the crater in the direction of Colony Two, waiting for any sign that the hybrids were coming for them. Understandable considering the situation, but what interested Jann was the fact the Kayden never once looked, like he wasn't in the least concerned. Perhaps he was made of stronger stuff. *He must have nerves of steel,* she thought.

When Jann finally stepped into Colony One and removed her helmet she took in a long deep breath. There was the familiar smell, a scent of home, fragrant and botanical. It sent her mind back to the very first time she opened her visor in Colony One, all those years ago. So much had happened, so much death, so much destruction. But soon she would be free of it, free of this place, free of Mars. Part of her would miss it, she knew that. Deep down she knew it owned a little bit of her now. How much she wasn't sure, but it was there all the same.

Her body itched and chafed inside the EVA suit and she could feel patches of ooze from the tank dried on to her flesh. She needed a shower, a very long shower to wash away the horror of her time in the recycling tank.

"Gizmo, can you show these guys where they can get some food and rest? I'm heading for the biodome."

"Certainly, Jann. May I say, it is good to have you back."

She smiled at the little droid. "It's good to be back, Gizmo." With that she stepped out of her EVA suit and ran into the garden. As she raced past the hydroponics and the food crops, she could see that Gizmo had been very diligent. All looked well tended to and lush. But it was different, more verdant than she remembered. She dashed across the central dais and dived headfirst into the pond, coming up again just under the waterfall. She felt instantly alive and full of vitality. She would wash the memory of Colony Two from her if it took all night.

IN THE END, it didn't last that long. Just half an hour or so. She had Gizmo bring her some fresh clothes and she sat in her old wicker recliner, drying her hair. It had grown quite a bit since the little robot had cut it off for her at this very spot.

"I have primed the fuel processing plant and it is now in production. I calculate thirty-four point two hours to complete the process. Then a further one point four three hours for filling and calibration."

"Excellent. Did you lock down all the airlocks like I asked?"

"It is done. No one can get in here without the use of heavy tools."

"And the others, what are they up to?"

"I took them into dome five and explained the procedure to them. They are taking it in shifts."

"Okay, good."

DOME FIVE HOUSED THE ARE, the Atmosphere Resource Extractor. This consisted of several units, each one dedicated to processing the thin Martian atmosphere and extracting various gasses from it, such as carbon dioxide, nitrogen, argon and even small amounts of oxygen. The area also housed the fuel processing plant. This took both carbon dioxide from the ARE and hydrogen from the SRE, the Soil Resource Extractor. The SRE was originally in dome five but had been moved by the early colonists down into the cave beneath the facility, the one that Jann entered when Nills had rescued her from the demented Commander Decker. It broke down the Martian soil into many components, one of which was water. This was further split into hydrogen and oxygen. Both units worked in tandem to provide Colony One with the essential resources needed to provide life support.

The dome also housed many other units that further combined these raw resources to create many more, one of which was methane—rocket fuel. This was manufactured by a chemical reaction between carbon dioxide and hydrogen. The resultant product was not stored inside the dome, but outside in a string of tanks that lined the exterior wall. There were several good reasons for this. One was simply to save space, but more importantly, methane would be highly dangerous stored in the oxygen-rich environment inside the colony, so it was safer to store it outside. As a result the process of filling the MAV tanks needed to be done by EVA, on the planet's surface.

As for the MAV fuel tanks, these were individually fabricated on trolleys, as once filled, they would be heavy, even in the one-third gravity of Mars. Each one needed to be wheeled out from dome five via an airlock, and moved into position to be filled, then a diagnostics routine run to check integrity. Once completed it would be parked out of the way so the next one could be processed. On top of this, there were several smaller oxygen tanks required. The combination of these two gasses created the propellant that would thrust the MAV off the surface and out of the Martian gravity well to rendezvous with the orbiter.

The whole process was slow and tedious, not designed for speed. So they had agreed to take it in shifts.

"WHO'S TAKING THE FIRST SHIFT?"

"Noome and Samir."

"Where's Kayden?"

"He is in the galley making tea."

"He's very calm, don't you think?"

"I do not think, Jann. I merely extrapolate."

Jann laughed—a long deep laugh. "Oh Gizmo, I've missed your quirky turn of phrase, and your blunt honesty. I never really appreciated it before now."

"I will take that as a compliment."

Jann sat back in the chair and looked around her. "I'll miss this place, too."

"What did you find in the mining outpost? I am curious to gather more data on it."

Jann sighed. "I found what I was looking for, a way to kill the bacteria."

"So you are no longer a biohazard?"

"No. It was a simple solution in the end. Expose it to a very high oxygen level at low pressure for around twenty-four hours. I don't know why I didn't think of it myself."

"Would you like me to initiate this procedure in the Colony One environment?"

"Oh god, yes. I had forgotten about it, what with everyone trying to kill me. But, yes, yes, absolutely, otherwise we'll be carrying it back with us."

"Should I inform the clones?"

"No, there's no need, and they're not clones, they are original colonists. Alphas, they call them." Jann sat up in the chair. "You know, Gizmo, there are hundreds of clones in Colony Two."

"Do tell me more."

"It's a vast cave system, with power generated from aero-thermal heat exchangers, a near limitless water supply, and a growing population. The whole shebang is run by Dr. Vanji, the original geneticist sent here by COM, and a small council of alphas."

"Sounds intriguing."

"The clones came from the analogues we saw in the research lab. These were the seeds they used to create their society, all in secret. No one outside this planet knows they exist."

"Even more intriguing."

Jann sat back in the chair again. "Well it's all messed up, if you ask me."

"Why is that?"

She leaned forward again and whispered. "Hybrids, Gizmo. They've created a new species of human. Not strictly clones, but an amalgam of enhanced human genetics. They call them Homo Ares."

"I have to admit, I am impressed."

"It's insane, Gizmo. Nobody should have that power. But that's not really the main problem. They are a form of super-human, with very strange behavior. The Council want to suspend the hybrid program, they're simply too scared of them. But Vanji is pursuing it, with ever more complex enhancements. They are his personal guard. They lay down the law in Colony Two, and watch out anyone who crosses him or his hybrids."

"So, who are these people with you?"

"Kayden is, was, on the council. Like a lot of the others, he became disillusioned with the way things were going, and he saw his chance to escape and return to Earth when I showed up."

"Because you know the launch sequence for the ISA MAV."

"As always, Gizmo, you are correct. I do."

"And the other two?"

"I don't really know. I only just met them a few hours ago. They're alphas, I'm pretty sure of that. But they're not on the Council, so they could be just some disgruntled colonists that Kayden recruited for his escape plan. They've been tracking the Odyssey and intercepting ISA comms for quite some time."

"Interesting."

"Look, Gizmo, I would love nothing better that to chat with you all night, but I have to get some sleep. It could get very hairy around here."

"Of course, Jann."

"What's our range on the perimeter scanner?"

"We can track surface movement up to approximately five klicks away."

She sighed. "Okay, alert me when anything shows up."

"Sounds like you are expecting company."

"Listen, Gizmo, I have a feeling they'll show up. Sooner rather than later. I don't care what Kayden says, they will come for us, hybrids most likely, so we need to be ready."

14

THE PURGE

Dr. Ataman Vanji sat at his study table, his face illuminated by a 3D projection of the planet Mars slowly rotating in front of him. It was rendered in high detail and showed the positions of all known satellites in orbit. Vanji zoomed in and examined one in particular. It wasn't a satellite, as such, it was the ISA Mars transit craft, Odyssey. Still faithfully waiting for the return of its crew, all these years later.

His ruminations were interrupted by the entrance of Xenon, his chief of security and the de-facto leader of the hybrids. He was tall, strong and elegant. He was a splendid specimen. Vanji allowed himself a faint smile as he admired his own work.

"Dr. Vanji, we have just received confirmation from Daniel Kayden. He is in situ in Colony One and has given a timeframe of thirty-six hours."

Vanji jumped up from his seat and clapped his hands

together. "Excellent. Then we have what we need to proceed."

"Is it time, then?"

Vanji wandered over to the balcony and looked out across the vast cavern. It was dimly lit now as it mirrored the Martin nighttime cycle. In less than an hour, though, dawn would break over the crater rim and a new day would begin.

"It is time, Xenon. Time to put our plan into action. Time to right the wrongs and take back the vision." He spun back. "How long to raise all the hybrids?"

"We are hive-mind, we speak as one, we gather quickly." He stopped, stood stock still and went into a momentary trance. The others on the Council all found this very disconcerting, but Vanji reveled in witnessing a hive-mind communicating.

Xenon returned from the trance and spoke. "We are ready."

"Then you know what to do. One group to round up all the council members and bring them here. The other group to eliminate the self-proclaimed leaders of the betas. Kill any who try to assist them. Is that clear?"

"It is clear." He turned on his heel and left Vanji to contemplate the coup he was now embarking on.

For too long had he compromised his vision, given in to consensus, bowed to the mewling for harmony. But no more. By dawn of this sol he would be master, free to pursue his experiments and all those who had thwarted him in the past would be pushed aside. *Recycling is too good for them,* he thought.

He walked out onto the balcony and looked down at the lush vegetation. A scream cracked the stillness, then another. He could just make out the faint, *phit, phit* of a railgun. "So it begins."

THE FIRST TO ARRIVE WERE HIS science team, three of them. They were the trusted few. They filed into the chamber in silence and took up positions beside Vanji, looking down over the cavern. "It won't be long now, then we will be free," said Vanji. The others nodded.

The door burst open and an ashen-faced Luka Modric rushed in, followed by two hybrids, who had now added railguns to their array of weapons.

"What is the meaning of this outrage? Have you gone mad?"

"Ahh, Luka, good of you to join us. Please, have a seat." He smiled and pointed at the council table.

Luka made a move towards Vanji, but he didn't get far. One of the guards raised a weapon at him. "Do as Dr. Vanji says and sit."

He stopped and a look of fear registered on his face as the realization of Vanji's ruthless arrogance finally sunk in. He sat down. By now more of the council members had been brought into the chamber, some willingly, some kicking and screaming, literally. Anyone who objected to this outrage or who put up any sort of a fight was cowed into submission by a few thousand volts jabbed into their ribs.

Finally, they were all assembled, meekly awaiting their fate.

"YOU MAY BE WONDERING why I called you all here," Vanji began. "Well, the reason is simple, it's time to move on."

"You have finally lost your mind, Vanji. This will not be tolerated. You are out of control." Luka stood up and shook a fist.

Vanji stayed quiet for a moment, then turned to one of the guards. "Would you mind if I borrowed that for a moment?" He pointed at the railgun the hybrid was holding. It used an electromagnet to fire a hard metal spike. It was not very accurate, but at close range it could release a projectile with enough force to penetrate a human skull. Vanji took the gun, aimed it at the hapless councilor—and fired.

A dull red blot appeared in the center of his forehead, his eyes rolled back and he collapsed on the floor, a pool of blood forming where he lay.

"Anyone else have anything to say?" Vanji swept the room with the gun. They were all silent. "I thought so. Good, I will continue then." He handed the railgun back to the hybrid.

"You all want to know what's going on? Well, here it is. It's very simple. I'm taking control of Colony Two. No more compromising my vision, no more pandering to the small-mindedness of the fearful. It is time to fully embrace the future. A future that belongs to the genetically superior. It is the very essence of evolution, it is nature's law and I intend to see it come to pass."

There was a momentary silence as the council members tried to comprehend the exact meaning of Vanji's words. Some were horrified, some were petrified, and some simply tried to understand how they didn't see this coming.

"So, members of the council, you are no longer required." With that he nodded to the hybrid leader and the room was filled, for a brief moment, with gunfire.

Some members died instantly. Some made a mad dash for the door, but never made it. After only a short few moments they were all dead. Vanji and his team of three geneticists were all that remained of the Colony Two council.

"And so it is done." He clapped his hands together and turned to the leader of the hybrids, Xenon. "The future of your species is now secure. I foresee a bright and productive time ahead for Homo Ares." With that, the light in the main cavern grew brighter. Vanji looked out at it. "Ah, a new dawn. How prophetic."

For a few moments they watched as the light grew brighter until the cavern was filled with a golden illumination.

"Xenon, have this mess cleaned up."

"Yes, Dr. Vanji."

"Now that we have accomplished this part of the plan, where are we with rounding up the beta leaders?"

Xenon entered his trance state as he communicated with the other hybrids. "They are putting up a fight. We have the main cohort corralled in the entrance cavern."

"How long before they are eliminated?"

"Not long. We will break through shortly."

"Good, get it done. We need to prepare the rover for departure as soon as possible."

"Yes, Dr. Vanji."

15

A NEW OLD FRIEND

Jann opened her eyes and had to think for a moment to establish where she was. Soft morning light illuminated her surroundings and she could hear the sound of a waterfall the background. She realized she was in the biodome of Colony One, and had fallen asleep in the wicker recliner after Gizmo had left. Jann breathed a gentle sigh of relief, stood up and looked around as she stretched her body. It was a beautiful morning in the biodome. And, compared to the horrors of Colony Two, it felt like heaven.

The familiar sound of Gizmo's tracked wheels burst through the vegetation, and zipped over to her. "Ah Gizmo, good morning."

"Sleep well, I trust?"

"Eh, no, not really, but it will do. Where are the others? Is it time for my shift?"

"Samir and Noome have just returned to rest. Kayden has been wandering around since first light."

"Really?"

"As far as I can tell. However, there is something that has come to my attention. I have picked up a rover, traveling this way, about five klicks out."

"Shit, when?"

"Just now."

"Have you told the others?"

"Not yet."

Jann thought about that. "This is not good. How much time before it gets here?"

"Twenty two point seven minutes, approximately."

"Dammit. Tell the others, we had better get ready."

Gizmo whizzed off as Jann raced for the operations room.

She stood over the holo-table looking at a 3D rendering of the Jezero Crater. At the very edge of its range a small orange icon marked the location and progress of the rover. The others had all gathered around to watch.

"We don't have much time," said Jann.

"This is bad, this is so bad, we're all dead," said Noome.

"I thought you said the rovers were all disabled?" Jann directed her question at Kayden, who had been silent since entering the operations room.

"I said they hadn't worked in years," he replied,

without taking his eyes off the slowly moving orange marker. "I genuinely didn't think this would happen."

"What? That they wouldn't try and stop us from leaving Mars?"

He looked over at Jann, and back to the marker, shaking his head. "It doesn't make any sense."

"We're all going to die," offered Noome.

"Noome, for God's sake, would you get a grip," Samir shouted at her.

Jann looked at the marker for a moment. "Seems strange. Not because they're coming after us, but because they haven't deactivated the rover beacon."

"What do you mean?" Samir had now progressed to comforting Noome, as anger didn't seem to work.

"Think about it. If you were planning to go after us, you wouldn't advertise it, would you?"

The others looked at the marker as if this revelation from Jann would somehow transform it into something more benign.

"No, I suppose not. But maybe they don't know about the beacon?"

"What are we going to do?" said Noome.

"We hide, that's what we do."

"Hide, are you kidding me?"

"Trust me, I have the perfect place. We can make them think we've left the facility. That way, when they start to scatter to search, we pick them off, one by one."

"Hide sound goods to me," said Noome.

"They'll find us for sure," said Kayden.

"No, I doubt it. When the ISA crew came here first, Nills Langthorp hid out. We never would have found him until he wanted to be found. It's our best chance."

"Wait," said Gizmo. He raised a metal hand and twisted his head like he was looking off into the distance. "They are transmitting." He raced over to the comms desk and tapped a few times on the control pad. Radio static crackled around the Operations room.

"...two injured, need medical assistance, over."

They stood in silence for a moment, looking at the comms desk.

"Colony One, this is Lars-beta, we have two injured, need medical assistance, over."

Jann moved over to the comms desk and pressed transmit.

"This is Dr. Jann Malbec, Colony One. State your purpose."

"Jann Malbec, am I really talking to you?"

Jann looked around at the others and raised an eyebrow.

"Yes you are, now state your purpose."

"We escaped the colony. There's been a coup, many dead, we have two injured and we need help."

"It's a trap, a trick to get us to let them in," said Samir.

"Well, there's no point in hiding, they know we're here now," said Kayden.

"What do you mean coup?" Jann continued.

"The hybrids started rounding up council members this morning. I think they're all dead. Then they went after the leaders

of the betas. We fought back, got trapped in the main entrance cavern... we escaped... the others in there... I don't know."

"Christ, I knew it, I knew this would happen, sooner rather than later. Those bastards, they were getting weirder by the day." Samir was stomping around.

"Kayden, you have any thoughts on this, since you're a council member?"

"Eh... well I'm shocked. If it's true, that is."

"Shocked? Is that it, you're *shocked*?"

Kayden raised his hands. "What do you want me to say? Yes, I'm shocked. And it looks like we got out just in time."

Jann turned back to the comms desk.

"Have you got EVA suits?"

There was a pause, presumably they were checking. This was a good sign as far as Jann was concerned. If they were lying then the response would be instant.

"We've got one, wait..." there were some indistinct snippets of conversation in the background. *"...shit, it's got no power..."* more background talk, *"We have two injured, one I don't think could EVA, even if we had a suit... and there's another problem... we have less than twenty minutes of air left in the rover."*

"Hang in there, we'll think of something."

"They could just drive in to the workshop garage, there's air in there." Samir had calmed down a bit.

"There's no way through from there, they would still have to EVA."

"You're not seriously thinking of letting them in?" said Noome.

"Look, this is actually good news for us. Because if they are who they say they are, then that means we have both rovers and no one can come after us, unless they walk."

"Boateng-beta walked here."

"Yeah, and it killed him," said Samir.

"I say we do as Samir suggests and send them to the workshop. We can keep them corralled in there. It would be safer, for all of us," said Kayden.

"There is another option," said Gizmo, as it moved over to the holo-table and brought up a 3D schematic of the Colony One facility and zoomed in on one sector.

"This module has an airlock that connects with the one on the back of the rover. They simply reverse it up close, and we can manipulate the umbilical to connect."

Jann looked at the 3D image. "Does it still work?"

"Well that could be a problem. Nills built a windmill in it, back during the sandstorm, so it is full of dust and debris. It would need to be cleaned out and checked. But my analysis suggests that should take only a few minutes."

"Okay, let's do it."

JANN SENT a message to the stricken rover and gave them instructions where to go and what to do. Then she,

Noome and Samir suited up to EVA. Kayden was left to operate the airlock from inside Colony One.

As they stepped out on to the planet's surface they could already see the rover in the distance. Gizmo raced off to direct it to the airlock. Jann and the others made their way there and started to clear out the sand blocking the outer door. They had disconnected the windmill and had cleared out most of the debris when the rover pulled up. Dust blew up around them as Gizmo directed them in. They backed up slowly and the rover inched its way along the guide rails to within operating distance of the airlock. Jann and Noome stepped into the open door and manually hoisted the connecting umbilical. It clicked into place at the rear of the rover with a satisfying clunk.

"Kayden, you can pressurize it now."

"Okay." His reply echoed in her EVA suit helmet. She waited... and waited.

"Christ, Kayden, what's the problem, these guys are breathing nothing but CO_2 by now."

"I'm trying, I'm trying... it's not working."

"Dammit, we've got to do something." With that Jann could feel a noticeable vibration in the airlock and it began to pressurize."

"Wait, it's just started working... that's weird."

"I did a manual override from the control panel on the outside. That is why it is working," said Gizmo.

The alert flashed green and Jann popped the visor on her helmet. The rear door of the rover cracked open and out came two betas, one supporting another who looked badly injured. She had a blood-drenched bandage around her thigh, her face was ashen.

"Thank you, we were dying in there." The beta's eyes widened, "Are you Dr. Jann Malbec?"

"Yes, come on. Let's get you all to the medlab."

"I am honored." He bowed.

"Quick, Noome, help get them inside."

Finally the last beta came out of the rover, his arm was in a sling and he had blood spatter on his face, but there was no mistaking who he was. Jann recognized him immediately.

"Nills! Is that really you?"

He looked at her and smiled. "Yes, I am Nills-beta."

Jann's face betrayed a look of astonishment. He really did look exactly like the Nills she used to know—the same bright smile, the same raggedy chin, the same unkempt hair.

"You knew my alpha, didn't you?"

"Yes, a long time ago now, he... he was a dear friend to me."

16

MEMORIES

"Are they all dead?" Kayden directed his question at Nills who was now sitting on a bed in the Colony One medlab.

"I don't know, it all happened so fast."

"And what about Vanji and the science team?"

Nills shrugged. "I don't know."

"Christ, this is insane," said Samir.

"Well, it looks like we got out not a moment too soon." Kayden patted Samir on the shoulder.

"So you're the one who helped Dr. Jann Malbec escape."

"Yeah, we all did." Kayden waved a hand over at Noome who was tending to the injured beta.

"Why? You're a council member, you had a lot to lose."

"Not any more, it would seem. If what you're saying is true."

"You'd better believe it. The hybrids control Colony Two now."

"Greetings Nills, glad to have you back." Gizmo raced into the medlab followed by Jann who had divested herself of her EVA suit.

"Eh... this is Gizmo, Nills. You built him."

Nills looked quizzically at the droid. "You mean my alpha did."

"Yes."

Nills scratched his chin. "I have no memory of this machine."

"Gizmo was built after the analogues of the colonists were created. So, assuming that was the source for the cloning, then you would have no knowledge of it."

Nills continued to stare intently at the robot.

"Would you like me to fetch you some tea?"

Nills laughed. "Sure, yes, why not." Gizmo raced off.

"That's an amazing machine. And you say my alpha designed it?"

"Yes. He did have a lot of time on his hands."

Nills shook his head and then looked around the medlab. "I have memories of this place. Dreams. I remember the layout."

"Here, let me have a look at that arm." Jann unclasped his hand from his upper arm and inspected the wound. It was superficial. She went off to get some bandages and saw Lars looking around in awe at the place. "Lars?"

He stood up and bowed. "Dr. Malbec."

"Do you know where the galley is?"

He thought about this for a moment. "I do, I have memories of it."

"Then why don't you go there and help Gizmo prepare some food. We'll have it in the common room. You know where that is too, don't you?"

His eyes went wide. "I do, I know this place, as if I've been here before."

"Good, then you know what to do."

When Jann returned to Nills, he was explaining all of what he knew about the hybrid coup to Samir and Kayden.

"When they had finished with the council members they came after us, the beta leaders. It was very early so most of us were still asleep. But we were down in the main entrance cavern. You see, when you guys escaped we were sent down to check on the readiness of the second rover and to see if any of the other vehicles were operational. That's when we heard the news that the hybrids had gone on the rampage. We barricaded ourselves in, but they were too strong and broke through just as we were making run for the rover. They killed six of us in the first charge. Two were injured, we're all that made it out."

"Those bastards." Samir turned to Kayden. "How come you didn't see this coming? You're on the Council."

"Nobody saw it. Do you think any of those on the council who are now dead saw this coming?"

Noome had finished patching up Anika, who sat up on the edge of the bed looking pale. "Well, it doesn't matter now anyway, we're leaving this godforsaken rock forever."

"Leaving?" Nills stood up.

"Yeah, we have a ticket for the next bus, and I for one, am taking it."

"You mean leave Mars, go back to Earth? How?"

"The old ISA MAV," said Jann. "The one I came here in. It's still operational and the Odyssey transit craft is still in orbit, waiting for it to return. I can go back."

"To Earth?"

"Yes, but not for at least another sol. The fuel tanks aren't ready yet." She turned to the others. "We're safe here for the moment, the hybrids have no way to get to us.

"Jann's right, there's no panic," said Kayden.

"Come on then, let's eat." One by one, they shifted out of the medlab into the common room.

GIZMO AND LARS had been busy. The table was arrayed with standard colony fare. Fruit, fish and, if Jann wasn't mistaken, colony cider. They all sat and picked at the food. No one spoke much, it had the feeling of a last supper. The mood was somber. After a while it was Nills who finally broke the silence. "I was wondering, if you have time before you leave, would you show us the biodome?"

"Sure, we have plenty of time now," said Jann. "You probably have a memory of it."

"We do, but I'd like you to show it to us, if that's okay with you all?" He turned to Kayden who just opened his hands. "Sure, go ahead."

The betas all rose. Lars helped Anika as Jann led them toward the biodome. She felt like she was bringing pilgrims on a tour of some sacred site. *Maybe that's how they see it*, she thought. They stopped just inside the entrance and craned their necks to take it all in.

"Wow, I can't believe I'm really here. It's exactly how I dreamed it would be." Lars could not contain his awe. The experience of standing in the biodome of Colony One was visibly emotional for him. Anika too, seemed mesmerized.

"Come on, let me show you the central dais, it used to be my home. I slept in a tree, can you believe that?"

None of them replied, obviously anything Dr. Jann Malbec did was okay with them. Jann was conscious that Anika was finding walking painful. "Here, why don't you sit down in my recliner and rest that leg."

Anika was open mouthed for a moment. "Are you sure that's okay? I mean, I would be occupying your seat."

"Of course, sit." Anika lowered herself into the wicker recliner and looked decidedly uncomfortable at her sacrilege. A mere mortal desecrating the temple of a deity.

"It's okay, sit, I insist."

"You are too kind, Dr. Malbec."

"Don't be silly, you're injured, you need it more than I do."

"Lars, would you keep Anika company here, while Dr. Malbec and I take a quick tour?"

"Of course."

Nills-beta signaled to Jann to take a walk with him. When they were out of earshot he spoke. "You must forgive them, they see you as a deity. A god, if you will."

"I've noticed it already, in Colony Two, the bowing and deference. I feel somewhat unworthy of such consideration."

"It's just the dreams we betas have, they can do strange things to the mind."

"What are they like, these dreams?"

"They are fragments of retained memory, from our alphas, like snippets of encoded experience. At first they are vague, but as we age they become like memories. Memories of places we have never seen, of things we have never touched, of events we have never experienced."

"Is it not difficult to deal with this... retained memory?"

"It is. For some it can be just too much, too confusing. They go insane. Others manage them by creating myths. Like, of this place. We all have memories if it. I can tell you the exact layout of Colony One even though this is the first time I've set foot in here."

"So why am I so special to them?"

"Colony One has become an Eden, or Nirvana, or Heaven. Betas have developed a near religious perception of this place. Some believe it doesn't really exist, it's just, literally, a figment of the imagination. When you showed up, it was like an angel had descended amongst them. A deity who had journeyed from the mythical Colony One. You can see how this would affect some of them."

"I see. I should never have gone there. None of this would have happened if I had just stayed put."

"Why did you come?"

"Oh it's a long story. I was looking for a way out, a way to go home."

"And did you find it?"

"Yes, I found it. Now I can go, get back to Earth."

"But you're still here."

Jann laughed. "Sorry, but you remind me so much of Nills. It's the sort of thing he would say."

Nills-beta smiled. "I'll take that as a good thing, then."

"Please do, he was a very good friend and... I've missed him... all these years."

THEY WALKED for a bit in silence. Then Jann stopped and looked at him for a moment. "Tell me, Nills, what are you going to do now?"

"I'm going back."

"But why? It's extremely dangerous. God knows what's going on in Colony Two by now."

"They're my people, I'm their leader. Without me they will be turned into slaves for Vanji's hybrid army."

"You think Vanji is still alive? You think he is behind all this?"

"You met him, what do you think?"

"I don't know, it's possible. But those hybrids are a very strange species. It's hard to know what they think. If you go back, you would most likely be captured and killed. It would do no good."

"If I were to return with you, then the betas would fight. They might rally behind me, but they would lay down their lives for you."

Jann stopped for a moment as the realization of what Nills was asking her sunk in. "You're asking me to go back there? Are you crazy?"

"Think about it. We outnumber them, seven or eight to one. All they need is the will to fight. You can give them that will."

"But how?"

"Your mere presence. The fact that you have returned, in their darkest hour. All those myths become real, they would be a formidable fighting force. They can win their freedom, all because you have returned."

"I... I need to think... I can't comprehend this all now... we're leaving, for Earth. Home, Nills, I'm going back home."

17

DECISION TIME

J ann sat in the recliner on the central dais of the Colony One biodome and considered her options. Nills had left her there to think about his request, Lars and Anika had followed him out. So she was alone now, with her thoughts.

She had everything she needed to return home. She was no longer a biohazard, the MAV was waiting, all her ducks were lined up. Kayden and his crew couldn't leave without her as she was the only one who knew the launch sequence, and now that both rovers were at Colony One, the hybrids couldn't journey here that quickly, so she had time to think.

EARTH, to walk in the sunshine, to feel the wind in her hair, to get wet in the rain. It was the simple things she missed. Humans were designed for Earth, it was their planet, home. She had dreamed of it for so long, but now that the time had come, she hesitated. What would await her there? She, along with Kayden, Noome and Samir, would be the only humans ever to have returned from Mars. Many had gone but none had returned, so far. No doubt she would become a celebrity of sorts. Shunted around from one interview to another. Sell her story, want for nothing. They would be bringing back with them stories of Colony Two and the miraculous advances in genetic engineering that had been made there. Human cloning, genome manipulation, the secret of immortality. They would be returning with tales of Eldorado, the city of gold, of riches beyond your wildest dreams. And like the adventurers of old, there would be no shortage of private funding for return missions. Every mega-corporation the world over would pump money into *Mars stocks*, betting on who would be the one to return this life-saving technology to Earth.

And whose life would it be saving? It wouldn't be the poor, or the downtrodden, or those on the margins. It would be the preserve of the very wealthy. The rich would have eternal youth, a new strata of super-elite would be created.

Then, there was the fact that Earth had left her for dead up here. No funding available for a rescue mission for her, she was expendable. What was the cost of her life? Not that she could blame them, really. After all, she was in no danger of dying and the popular consensus of the general population was there were better things to

GERALD M. KILBY

spend taxpayer's money on than rescuing a foolhardy astronaut. She knew the risks, she would have to live with the consequences.

HER OTHER OPTION was to go with Nills, back to Colony Two. To what? Death, the horror of the recycling tank? His assertion that her presence would galvanize the betas into revolution seemed nothing more than fantasy to her, simply wishful thinking on his part. Jann could not see any way that they would get more than two feet inside Colony Two before they were killed.

As for the plight of the betas, she had no doubt that they revered her in some way, but would that be enough to overcome well-armed hybrids, no matter how much they outnumbered them? They were timid and deferential by nature, or maybe nurture, either way she doubted they had the collective balls to put up a fight.

So what would be their fate then? Subjugation, slavery, genocide? It would be one of them. At best they would be domesticated humans, used as beasts of burden, workhorses for the superior species that was Homo Ares. Did they deserve that? They might be clones but they were still human, and Homo sapiens at that, her species.

And what of Vanji? Was he still alive? And if so, what was his game plan? She had the distinct feeling that somehow, he must be behind all this. He wanted to create his advanced race without hindrance or moral sermons from the council members. But then again he could be dead, along with the others. And why should she care? What were they to her that she should forgo her one chance of returning to Earth?

She also had a third option. Stay here in Colony One and take her chances. She sighed, stood up from the recliner, and walked over to where she kept some of her personal belongings. It was a storage box she had refashioned into a kind of table. She opened it up and pulled out a small holo-tab. It was her ISA mission manual, it had everything she needed to launch the MAV and return to Earth. She shoved it into a pocket on the side of her flight suit and headed out of the biodome, probably for the very last time.

18

READY TO LEAVE

"W here's Nills?" Jann entered the common room to find Kayden sitting at the table. The remains of half-eaten plates of food were scattered around it like the aftermath of a party. Kayden looked up. "The robot is giving him a tour."

Jann relaxed. "Okay."

"Are you ready? We need to start helping with the tanks, time is marching on," he said.

"Not yet. I need to show you this first." She took the holo-tab out of her pocket, cleared some space on the table and switched it on. Icons danced in the air above its surface, she tapped one and a 3D rendering of the MAV was displayed. She tapped again and a schematic of one of the fuel tanks broke off from the main diagram. "As you know, the fuel tanks are built on trolleys. Once they're all filled and checked they can be connected together, like a train, and the rover will pull the whole lot over to the MAV."

Kayden nodded.

"Each trolley has a hydraulic arm to lift them individually into position. They fit in like this." She tapped the 3D rendering of the tank. An animation played showing how it locked into position on the MAV and detailed the connecting points. "Once you've got them all into position you open the valves here, using this exterior control panel."

"Okay, looks straightforward."

"It is, it was designed that way. Nothing too fiddly to operate wearing EVA suit gloves." She tapped the MAV again and this time it zoomed in to the cockpit.

"You enter the MAV through this hatch here. Over on the main console is the switch that activates the MAV power system. Once you flip that on, the flight dash should light up like a Christmas tree. Tap the main screen and it will ask you to enter a code. The code is four zeros."

"Four zeros?" asked Kayden incredulously.

"It doesn't need high security. Let's face it, who the hell is going to steal it out here?"

"Makes sense. Go on," said Kayden.

"The MAV will then run a diagnostic routine on all flight systems. You can override any alerts, unless they are mission critical. Assuming all goes okay, it will then try to contact the Odyssey."

"The orbiter?"

"Yes. The launch is controlled from the Odyssey computer systems. It's all automatic, you don't have to do anything from that point on, just sit back and wait."

"How long?"

"Hard to say, could be a few minutes, could be a few hours."

"Hours?"

"Yes, the Odyssey orbits every five hours, so depending where it is you may have to wait. It will calculate the launch time to intercept."

"That could be a long wait."

"Once the MAV makes contact and the trajectory is worked out, it will start to count down. Then you'll know how long." Jann tapped another icon and the 3D image was replaced with a diagram of the Odyssey in orbit around Mars. "Once you reach the correct altitude the Odyssey will also automate docking. You don't have to do anything."

"I like that bit," said Kayden.

"Lastly. Now that the MAV has docked, the Odyssey knows to prepare for return to Earth." She tapped the rendering of the spaceship and the view zoomed into the flight cockpit. "You'll get confirmation on the main console here. Now, you may feel that nothing is happening, because the EM Drive is pretty slow to get going, but it will be accelerating the craft through a number of orbits until it reaches escape velocity and... well, next stop Earth."

Kayden was silent for a moment, looking at the

projection and nodding. Then he sat back and looked at her. "Tell me, why did you never return before now? You could have left any time."

Jann rubbed the top of her head; her hair had grown quite a bit so it no longer had that soft velvety feel to it. "I couldn't. I was a biohazard, remember?"

"Even so, you could have just gone, taken the risk, what could they do once you arrived in Earth orbit?"

"Blow me out of the sky, most likely. Or at best, if they actually let me land, contain me in a hermetically sealed bubble, where I would spend the rest of my days being poked and prodded by scientists. No thank you. I'd rather stay here."

Kayden nodded. "Yeah, I see your point."

"Which reminds me. I need to send a report back, let them know the MAV is returning. I'd like to be a fly on the wall when they hear the news about Colony Two, and all that."

"I would suggest holding off on that for the moment. We can do it from the orbiter. We haven't lifted off yet, so best not to tempt fate."

"Don't tell me you're superstitious."

Kayden laughed. "No, it's not that... just... I think it would be better. After all, we still have to persuade them that we're not carrying back the pathogen."

Jann thought about this. "Well, I'll leave it up to you. It doesn't matter to me now anyway. I'm not coming with you." Jann switched off the holo-tab and handed it to Kayden. "Here, this is all you need."

"Not going? But this is your chance to go home, isn't that what you wanted?" Kayden looked shocked.

"I thought I did, but you know what? I decided I like it here."

"You may never get another chance."

"So be it." She waved a dismissive hand.

Kayden stood up, clutching the holo-tab with both hands. "If you change your mind, you know where we are."

"I won't, but thanks."

He stood for a moment, just looking at her, before nodding and walking out of the common room.

JANN SAT for a while before she noticed Nills-beta standing in the doorway of the galley. "How long have you been there?"

He moved over to her and sat down. "Long enough."

So you heard all that?"

"All that I needed to. You're not going back to Earth, then?"

"No."

"Why?"

"Does it matter?"

"No, I don't suppose it does. So what now?"

"You tell me."

"A little counterrevolution, maybe?"

"Count me in. When do we start?"

"I think we already have."

19

WEAPONS

Nills-beta wandered around the main Colony One workshop, examining the various artifacts scattered over every available surface. Part of him felt like he was intruding on the sacred space of a dead relative, a feeling that held some validity. But part of him also felt like he was home, such was the familiarity he had with this workshop. His alpha had worked here, probably where he built the small robot, Gizmo, that now seemed to have attached itself to him. Feeling perhaps that its creator had at long last returned and, like a faithful dog, was not going to let him out of its sensory range again.

"It is just like old times, Nills," said Gizmo.

Nills cocked an eyebrow at the eccentric machine, marveling at its creator's skill. The very same skill that lay within him. The original Nills had attained legendary status amongst the betas. It was rumored he was still alive, which made Nills-beta the only clone of a living alpha. This made him someone special within the colony and, in a sense, leadership had been foisted on him rather than acquired by rite. That, and the extraordinary engineering skills that he had inherited all added to his prominence in the community. *'There was just something about him,'* was the oft-used refrain. But how much of this was valid, and how much was simply amplified by the myths and legends that propagated through beta society, was anyone's guess. Nonetheless, without the creation myths they would never have had the spiritual strength to contend with their dreams, their memories, their ethereal past.

It was this same spiritual affinity that he was banking on when they returned to Colony Two. That, and the hope that Dr. Jann Malbec's return would galvanize the betas to foment revolution. If he was the de facto leader, then she was the spiritual leader. But again, this was by dint of myth rather than physical reality. Not that it really mattered. If it worked then... good. If not then... so be it.

JANN HAD GONE off with Lars to prepare the rover and EVA suits, they needed everything to be working at a hundred percent if they were to have a chance. Kayden and the alphas had decamped to dome five to get ready for their own departure back to Earth. He gave them no more thought, good luck to them.

That left himself, Gizmo and the injured Anika. His

own injuries were minor and healing fast. Anika, however, had sustained a more serious injury from a railgun dart in her upper right thigh, but that too was healing fast and she was already able to put some weight on the leg. Hopefully she would be able to join the fight.

If they were to have any chance of gaining access into Colony Two then what they needed were weapons. Nills and Anika scanned the area for anything they could use. Simple heavy bars or knives were not going to be enough, they needed to manufacture something more lethal, and quickly.

"So what are we looking for, Nills?"

"Coils, capacitors, anything we can make railguns out of."

"What about explosives? They seem to be very popular in human wars," offered Gizmo.

"Yeah, now you're talking, Gizmo. What have you got in mind?"

"I am eighty-six point seven percent certain I can concoct something usable from the chemicals we have here in Colony One."

"Excellent, get to it then."

"Which would you prefer? Explosive, incendiary or smoke?"

Nills looked at Gizmo. "I suppose all three might come in handy."

"Aye, aye, captain." And it whizzed off out of the workshop.

"How does it know all that stuff?" Anika was watching

the little robot disappear off into the bowels of Colony One.

"I really have no idea."

"But you created it."

"Not me, my alpha."

"But there is a little bit of you in that robot, nonetheless."

"Perhaps. All I can say is, it's a damn handy machine to have around."

They continued their search, picking up parts as they went and dropping them into a handcart that Nills was pulling.

"This looks useful." Anika picked up a bank of electromagnetic coils.

Nills examined it. "Good, see if you can find some more, and capacitors, lots of great big ones."

After a half hour or so they cleared a space on one of the workshop tables and dumped all the components onto it. They were making railguns. Similar to those used by the hybrids but these would be significantly cruder. Railguns are electrically powered from batteries, which charged a bank of capacitors to around 1000v. When the trigger is pulled this activates a row of toroidal electromagnets, each one accelerating a metal projectile along the rail.

Nills and Anika toiled away at their task. Fortunately she was also a talented engineer and had no problem crafting sophisticated machines from a bucket of spare parts. This was how most things in Colony Two were made. Nothing was wasted, everything reused and recycled. Even humans.

AFTER A FEW HOURS of intensive fabrication, Jann and Lars finally returned.

"Rover is fully fueled and supplied, EVA suits are patched up and ready to use. How are you getting on here?"

Nills looked up from the bench where he was soldering a component. "Nearly ready for testing." He waved away the smoke that was corkscrewing up from the joint. He picked up the railgun, flicked a switch to charge it, and inserted a sharp metal spike in the breech. He stood up. "Stand back."

Everyone moved aside as Nills aimed the weapon at a disemboweled refrigeration unit about fifteen meters away and pulled the trigger. It fell over with the impact as a shower of fragments exploded from the entry point.

"I think that should do the trick." Nills examined the weapon and placed it back down on the bench. "We've made two of these, this one and a smaller unit that Anika is finishing."

She appeared from behind a mound of parts. "I also made this." She held up a small crossbow, fitted a short metal arrow in it and fired it at the remains of the refrigeration unit. It buried itself deep in the machine.

"Excellent," said Nills.

"Where's Gizmo?" Jann looked around the workshop.

"He's off conjuring up a batch of explosives." Nills picked up a small spherical container from a mound of similar objects. "We can make some grenades out of these."

"Looks like we're nearly ready," said Lars.

"In that case I'd better go and get my weapon," said Jann.

"You have one?"

"Oh yes, and I'm pretty good with it too." She turned and headed out of the workshop.

They continued to test the weapons for a while before Gizmo finally showed up with several containers. It placed them carefully on the floor, moved back and then extended a metal hand, pointing at them, one at a time.

"This will give you an explosion, this flame, and this one here, smoke." It then carefully opened the last box. "I have also utilized these small glass vials from the medlab." Gizmo held one up to the light. It was a standard sealed glass capsule. "You can use these as fuses. They are somewhat crude, but when this breaks open, the chemical inside will start the reaction in these others. Just be careful you do not do it by accident. Otherwise… boom." It made a sweeping move with its arms, to emphasize the point.

"That's great work, Gizmo. Thank you."

"My pleasure, I am here to assist."

. . .

As they gathered around the workbench and started to fabricate the grenades, Nills was beginning to feel more confident. Now that they had some weapons, they might be able to hold out long enough for the betas to get behind them. But even armed to the teeth, if they didn't, all this would be in vain. No amount of clever engineering would save them then. They were just finishing the last of them when Jann returned carrying a bunch of long metal spikes. Lars looked over at her. "I thought you were getting a weapon."

Jann looked around the workshop wall. It was a large space, maybe fifty meters across. "See that chart pined to the wall down there?"

They all looked up from their work and across to where Jann was pointing. It was a small paper chart of some kind. Something a former colonist stuck there for some long forgotten reason.

"Yeah," said Lars.

Jann placed the spears on the ground, sorted through them and selected one. She hefted it above her head and launched it at the target. It split the air at an impressive speed and buried itself, dead center in the chart. It was a good thirty meter throw.

"Wow," said Nills.

"That's amazing," said Anika. "Where did you learn to do that?"

Jann was walking back down the workshop to retrieve the projectile. "Oh, I had a lot of time on my hands here."

She returned with the spear. "Want to see something else?"

"Sure," said Lars.

"Gizmo, would you be so kind?"

"You are not going to do this. I thought we were friends again."

"We are, Gizmo. I just want them to see."

"Oh, all right then." Gizmo whizzed a few meters away from Jann.

"Ready?" said Jann.

"Gizmo is always ready."

She launched the spear directly at the little robot's head. Before any of them had time to think, Gizmo simply grabbed it out of the air.

"Wow, how can it do that?" said Anika.

"Ultra-fast reflexes," said Jann. "Pretty impressive, don't you think?"

"Incredible," said Nills.

"I have a request," said Gizmo.

"Sure, what is it?"

"I would like to join you on your adventure."

Nills and Jann exchanged glances. "It will be dangerous, Gizmo."

"You are forgetting I am a robot, that is meaningless to me. I have extrapolated that being alone is less simulating than being in the company of friends." It moved its head and looked from Nills to Jann. "And you are my friends."

Nills walked over to the robot and put his hand on its

metal shoulder. "I, for one, would be glad to have you along."

"I would consider it an honor," said Jann.

Gizmo looked up at its friends and if it could smile it would have had the broadest grin ever seen on a robot.

When the moment had passed Nills turned back to them. "Okay, I think we're ready."

"So what's the plan?" Jann was taking the spear back from Gizmo's metal hand. The others all looked at Nills.

"Let's get some food and we can discuss it."

THE PLAN, such as it was, revolved around the assumption that Jann's return to Colony Two would rouse the betas. Since they outnumbered the hybrids and the few remaining alphas, they could, in theory, take control. But it was evident to Jann that there were a number of gaps in this plan. First and foremost, would the betas be inspired into action, as Nills had asserted? He was convinced, but Jann was not so sure. Second, did they have the strength of arms, the weapons? And third, it assumed that the situation hadn't changed since their escape. In truth, they didn't really know what was going on. What was the end game? Was it being instigated solely by the hybrids, and if so, what was their motivation? Or was there more to it? Was Vanji involved, was he behind it? All these questions they could not answer.

Into this mix were the three alphas in Colony One who were now diligently working away in dome five, preparing the fuel and oxygen tanks for the ISA MAV. Getting ready to leave the planet for good. This struck Jann as somewhat of a coincidence. Was there some relationship between these two events? Was there something else going on that none of them could yet see?

Then there was the very practical issue, how did they get in? And once inside, then what?

They had gathered themselves around the table back in the common room, and were all eating. It might be a while before they ate again so they might as well do it now while they still had the opportunity.

"So Nills, like I said, what's the plan?" Jann looked at him. He sat in the same battered armchair that the old Nills did. He had the same mannerisms and, if she didn't know better, she would think he was the same person.

"How about we drive up to the main entrance, blow it open with some explosives, charge in and start shooting any hybrids we see? Then, we just wing it from there."

"You're kidding me," said Anika.

Nills looked up from his food. "Of course I am, that's a really stupid idea."

Anika laughed. "For a minute there, I thought you were serious."

Nills set his bowl down on the table and sat back in his chair, like he always did. "For this to work, the betas need to know Jann Malbec has returned to free them, and call on all of them to raise up against the hybrids. So we need to get the word to them as soon as possible. Now, assuming life goes on in Colony Two, then the vast bulk of them will be working in the garden. So we need to get in there and hold it long enough for them to rally around."

"Okay, so how do we get in there?" Jann leaned in across the table.

"Yeah, that's not so easy, Nills. They're going to see us coming," said Lars.

"We need to give them the slip somehow, trick them into thinking we're entering by some other route."

"Would I be correct in assuming that their perimeter scanner is the same as the one in Colony One?" said Gizmo.

"I think so. I could check, as I'm very familiar with it. I used to fix it all the time," said Anika.

"Well if it is, then I may be of service."

"How so?" said Jann

"My systems are integrated with Colony One, so if they are the same, I may be able to access it and manipulate it."

"You mean, like hack into their systems."

"Partly. The downside, of course, is once I am out of range of Colony One I will not be able to access any of the systems here, so my data and processing capabilities will be dramatically reduced. I estimate by a factor of ten point seven two."

"Is that a lot?" said Lars.

"For me yes, but not so much that you would notice unless I had to do a complex extrapolation. In which case it would be glacially slow."

GERALD M. KILBY

"But you could access the Colony Two systems?"

"Only some, the perimeter scanner would be one. If it is the same as here."

"Okay, then. Sounds like we have a way in. We take the rover up close to the main entrance, park it there, and head on foot to the higher level escape airlock. Gizmo, can block their scanner until we're in."

"Is that the same airlock I used to get in?" said Jann.

"No, higher up. It's a bit of a climb, but it's never guarded and little known. We could get quite a way inside before encountering any hybrids."

"Sounds like we have a plan then," said Jann

They all nodded in agreement.

20

RETURN

By early the next morning, they had assembled in the workshop and organized themselves into teams, Jann and Gizmo, Nills and Lars. Anika was still injured so she kept the weight off her leg while she had the chance. It didn't take them long to get everything ready. Finally they assembled at the entrance to the airlock and got into their EVA suits.

"Should we say goodbye to the others?" said Jann

"Who?" said Lars.

"Kayden, Noome and Samir. After all, they were your colleagues."

"Screw them," said Anika. "If they want to run away, then let them."

"Well, they got me out of there, out of the tank. I can't go without thanking them, it's the least I can do."

"Hey, you've just given them the launch codes to the

only ship off this planet, so I'm sure they're pretty happy with you about that," said Lars.

"Go, be quick." Nills waved a hand. "Hurry."

Jann raced off.

"Gizmo, go with her, make sure she's okay."

DOME FIVE WAS CRAMMED with a myriad of flotsam and jetsam from the inventory of Colony One. At the far end Jann could see the crew busying themselves preparing to bring the last fuel tank out onto the surface. Samir and Noome were in EVA suits with their helmets off, while Kayden sat examining the data on the holo-tab that Jann had given him. She could see a 3D schematic of the landing site balloon out across the table from its surface.

"Change your mind?" Noome spotted her first.

"No, I just came to say goodbye. I'm going back with Nills and the others, back to Colony Two. We're ready to leave."

"Colony Two? Are you mad?" Noome looked at her, wide-eyed.

"Maybe." Jann shrugged. "I came to say thanks... for getting me out of that tank."

Kayden switched off the holo-tab, picked it up and waved it at Jann. "Thank you for this, it's our ticket off this godforsaken rock."

"I hope is works out for you," Jann replied.

"Tell me," Kayden put the holo-tab down and. "Are you really going back there?"

"Yeah, we're all tooled up, ready to go."

"It's probably a suicide mission, you know that."

"We'll see."

"They'll see you coming. How do you propose getting in? "

Jann thought about this question. Why was Kayden so interested? He was leaving, so what did it matter to him?

"We're not sure. I think we're going to drive up to the main entrance, blow a hole in it, charge in and start shooting... as far as I know."

"Sounds totally crazy to me." Samir started fiddling with a fuel valve.

"Yeah, does to me too. But anyway, thanks for getting me out... and, good luck." She turned.

"Good luck to you, too. I think you're the one who's really going to need it," said Kayden as Jann walked out of the dome.

NILLS and the other betas craned their necks to look out of the rover's window at the brooding Martian landscape. Jann realized that since they had lived their entire lives inside a cave, the outside world must be a wondrous spectacle to them. She looked out across the plateau towards the western rim of the crater. A thin haze of Martian dust clung to the atmosphere and colored the entire sky with a dark crimson wash. "Storm coming."

"How do you know?" said Nills.

She pointed out to the far horizon. "Dust darkens the sky when there's a sandstorm approaching." She looked back at him. "But don't worry, it won't hit here for a while yet."

She glanced at her navigation screen. "Coming up on six klicks. What's their scanner range?"

"Five, at most," said Anika.

"Okay, once we cross that boundary they can spot us. I sure hope you can hack that system, Gizmo."

"Hope does not enter into any of my calculations."

"Five point five klicks. We'll be in range in a minute or two. Are you ready, Gizmo?"

"I am always ready Jann."

She eased back on the throttle and the rover slowed to a crawl. They continued like this for a few more minutes. "Four point nine... eight... seven. How are we doing Gizmo?"

"Working on it."

"Four point five... should I stop?"

"Got it. Interesting... it appears to be an exact replica of Colony One's systems. Okay, there you go, disabled."

They looked at each other. "Are you sure? That seemed very easy."

"I am always sure, and yes, it was easy—when you know how," said Gizmo.

Jann pushed the throttle forward and the rover picked up speed. In the distance they could see the crater wall rise up from the horizon. Dust and sand billowed around them as they pushed on. She was driving the rover at the very edge of control. They were all bumped and jostled as the machine rumbled over the rugged terrain. Finally they came to a skidding halt, behind the same rocky outcrop that Jann had parked up at the first time she came here. It seemed like such a long time ago now, so much had happened to her since then. It was a very different Jann that entered Colony Two the first time. And here she was, doing it again.

She powered down the machine and turned around to look back at the others. They were getting their equipment ready. Nills prepared his railgun and checked the satchel containing the grenades Gizmo had fashioned. He had a determined look, and Jann realized this was a very different Nills. Not the carefree bohemian that tended plants and slept in a hammock. This Nills had had a different life, and it was beginning to show.

"Okay, listen up." Nills stood and held the railgun across his chest. "Show these bastards no mercy. They've killed the Council, probably most of the beta leaders and they are hell bent on the subjugation of our kin. They will not hesitate to kill us on sight. So don't mess around, you see one you kill them. Got it?"

Lars and Anika stood wide-eyed and looked a little sheepish. Even Jann had to admit, this was a whole new side of Nills she had never imagined. But in a way, he was being the person he needed to be, at this point in time.

"Got it," Jann replied.

"Pardon me, Nills. But who exactly are we killing? I am loath to admit it, but I am a bit confused," said Gizmo.

GERALD M. KILBY

"You don't kill anyone, okay Gizmo? You're a robot, leave any killing to us."

"Okay. No killing."

"Right, everyone ready?"

They checked their weapons, flipped down their helmet visors and moved out of the rover.

They kept low behind the rocky outcrop and followed the same path that Jann had taken previously. After a while they started to work their way up the side of the crater rim. They went in single file, Nills leading, picking a path up to the airlock that Jann had used. They stopped for a moment. Nills seemed to be studying the terrain.

"The path should lead to another airlock, farther up." He pointed towards a gentle rising slope strewn with rocks and boulders. "Stay close, keep each other in sight. If anyone falls behind, just shout out." He moved off, the others followed. They picked up the pace, all the time climbing higher until finally they came to a clear, level ledge. Just ahead, built into the cliff face, was the airlock. They approached it slowly, with caution.

"So far so good." Anika's voice echoed in Jann's helmet.

"Let's hope there isn't an army of hybrids waiting for us on the other side." Lars shuffled in behind Anika.

"There may be a few, so be ready." Nills checked his railgun. "Okay then, let's go."

He tapped on the airlock control panel and the outer door opened. They piled in, the door closed. "Well this is it," whispered Lars as they faced the inner door, weapons ready. The airlock pressurized and the door slid open to reveal an empty, dimly lit tunnel. They breathed a collective sigh of relief.

"There should be a storage room up to the right. We can get out of these suits in there. We'll be able to move better. Follow me." Nills led the way along the tunnel. It was little used. Jann noticed their footsteps leaving prints in the thick layer of dust along the floor.

"Here it is." Nills used the barrel of his gun to poke the door open. It was pitch black inside. Gizmo activated its headlight and spread the beam wide it to give 360 degree illumination. It was empty save for some low bench seating along the walls. Above these were tall empty racks.

"What is this place?" said Jann.

"Originally it would have contained EVA suits, to be used in an emergency by the miners working here. Anyway, it's a good place to dump these. Come on, let's hurry. Lars, keep an eye on the door while we get sorted, then we'll cover you."

They wasted no time in divesting themselves of the heavy suits and, when ready, Nills explained their options.

"This tunnel leads to the upper gallery around the top of the main cavern. Mostly this will be deserted save for the atmosphere recycling plant on the far side. That will have at least two, maybe three, betas working in it. If we can get there without being spotted, then we can alert them and get them to spread the word that Dr. Jann

Malbec has returned. I suggest we get the betas to assemble in the garden in the main cavern, that's where we'll have the most numbers. We'll need to get down there somehow and rally them, even if it means fighting our way there."

No one spoke. "Anybody got a better idea?" No one did. "Okay, then, let's go."

Nills led the way and they moved out in silence. Gizmo took up the rear.

After a short distance the tunnel opened onto a wider gallery. Nills and Jann took up positions on either side of the tunnel's end and peered around each corner. It was dark so it was hard to make anything out farther than a few meters. "Can't see shit." Jann whispered. Nills nodded to his right and stepped out in to the gallery, keeping his back to the wall. Anika and Lars followed, Jann and Gizmo brought up the rear.

Jann peered behind her into the darkness and thought she saw some movement. Then she heard a *thut.* Lars screamed and collapsed on the ground, grabbing his leg as blood oozed from the wound. Another *thut* and the rock wall beside Jann's head exploded into a hundred fragments. She loosed a spear into the blackness, aiming at nothing. Anika fired off a bolt before she too was hit. She spun around and went sprawling across the dirt floor.

"Shit, get down, down," Nills shouted at Jann as he tossed a grenade into the gloom and hit the deck. There was a blinding flash as the explosion shook the cavern.

The shockwave lifted Jann off her feet and sent her tumbling down the gallery. Rock and debris rained down all around her. Dust billowed out, filling the space. *Christ*, thought Jann, *We're being buried alive.*

After a few stunned moments she felt Nills' hand on her shoulder. "You okay?"

She spat and coughed. "Yeah. What the hell did Gizmo put in that?"

"I don't know, but any hope of stealth is gone, it must have taken down half the roof."

Jann spluttered, and spat again, trying to get the grit out of her mouth.

The dust began to clear a little and Jann could see a huge mound of rock blocking both the tunnel entrance and the galley walkway. "Christ, they're going to be all over us in a minute. We've got to move." She stood up and turned to see Nills kneeling over Lars. He was flat on his back, a pair of cold dead eyes staring up. He looked up at Jann and shook his head. He then turned to where Anika was lying. Her hand twitched, then moved, then she sat up slowly, feeling her chest as she rose. She dug a hand into a top pocket and pulled out a battery pack with a two inch long metal spike from a railgun embedded in it. "Shit, that was close. She threw it on the ground and stood up. "Lars?"

"Dead," said Nills.

"Lars, no, no..."

"Come on, there's no time. We've got to get out of here." Jann grabbed her arm and began to pull her along, then she stopped. "Shit, where's Gizmo?" She looked around and scanned the mound of rock that used to be the gallery roof.

"He must have gotten buried when the roof caved in," said Anika.

"No, Gizmo!"

"Forget it Jann. Let's get to the processing plant." Nills shouted.

Jann looked back at the last resting place of the eccentric robot. She had had a love hate relationship with it for more than three years. But now that it was gone, she felt like she had lost another true friend.

"Jann, for God's sake, let's move."

21

_____

REVOLUTION

Dust filled the air along the gallery. Every few meters light from the main cavern penetrated through long slits cut in the wall. Each slit had an extractor fan attached, making it one big air recycling duct, running most of the way around the upper level. The light flickered and danced off the walls and floor as the blades rotated.

Nills stopped suddenly and put his fingers to his lips. "Wait, hold up, I hear something," he whispered.

Jann could hear it too. Footsteps, running, coming toward them fast. Out of the gloom two figures burst into view, Anika fired off a shot, but missed, her bolt clanging off an extractor blade. The two figures stopped dead in their tracks. She was about to fire again when Nills shouted.

"Wait!" He ran forward. "Alban, sorry, are you okay?"

The figures stood wide-eyed. "Nills?"

"Yes, it's me."

"Nills, oh my god, we thought you were dead. What's going on? What are you doing here?"

"We can't talk here, hybrids will be coming."

"Those bastards, they've killed at least ten of us so far."

"Can we get to the recycling plant without being seen?"

They didn't reply. Instead they just stood there dumbly.

"Alban, can we get to the plant?"

"Dr. Malbec. You have returned." Alban stepped back and bowed, as did the other.

Jann came forward. "Yes, I have. Now, we must try to get to the main cavern without being seen."

"I know a way. Come, quick... follow me, hurry."

THE RECYCLING PLANT was one of two situated on the upper gallery of the vast main cavern of Colony Two. Their purpose was to regulate CO_2 and expel any excess out into the Martian atmosphere. It also maintained the level of moisture and humidity in its local area. There were two of these plants, working independently, to create different microclimates depending on the vegetation it was supporting. Dust and particulate matter was also extracted. The main difference between these air recycling systems and those used back on Earth was these used genetically engineered bacteria to get the job done, instead of a chemical process. The room was sizable but tightly packed with tanks and ducting, like the bowels of an oil refinery.

"This way." Alban led them through the maze to the far end of the room. He stopped in front of a large vertical duct and started to unbolt an inspection panel. "This leads down to the main cavern level. It's a tight fit but you should be able to shimmy down. We'll take the stairs, we can start to spread the word."

Jann stuck her head in through the gaping hole in the front of the duct and looked down. It was dark and the sides were lined with a thick layer of fine black dust. "It's a long way down. Got any rope?"

"No, sorry. You'll have to brace your back against one side, feet on the other and step down that way."

Nills was now poking his head into the duct and looking down.

"How many betas can we count on to join the fight?" said Jann as she shouldered the small crossbow.

"I'm not the only one in the colony that's sick of Vanji, and his experiments to create a master race of hybrids. But a lot will be frightened, some are emotionally fragile. You know this Nills, you don't need me to tell you."

"So, Vanji is behind all this?"

"You better believe it. Him and those weird hybrids of his."

"So, how many can we count on?" Nills had brought his head out from the duct opening.

"Hard to say. There's at least thirty that I know of who

would definitely take the opportunity to get rid of him. Others would follow if Dr. Malbec is in the mix, maybe sixty would fight."

"That's more than enough. Do you know where everyone is located?"

"At this time, the bulk will be in the main cavern. Vanji and the remains of the council are up in the chamber, big meeting."

"And the hybrids?"

"They're all over the place. Although, I know a cohort were heading for the entrance cavern a while ago."

"The entrance?" said Jann. "Any idea why?"

"Nope."

"Is that unusual?"

"Very, I've never seen them do that."

"We need to get moving before this place is overrun." Nills clambered into the duct. "It's a bit tight in here."

"That's probably a good thing, it will stop you falling too far when you slip," said Anika.

JANN WAS last to enter the duct. Nills went first, then Anika. As soon as she was sure of her footing, Alban closed up the inspection panel and the space became pitch-black, save for a very distant light, far below.

They moved slowly, feeling their way. Every three meters or so, the ducting was clamped together, affording a little ledge to place the edge of a foot. In other places it was joined by more ducts heading off at right angles.

These junctions gave them a little respite from the long slow descent. Jann could hear Anika wince as they moved, her injured leg was taking a lot of strain. In the distance they could hear the muffled sounds of running and clamoring voices. The hybrids were racing up to the gallery where the explosion took place. So far no one had opened the inspection panel above Jann's head. They kept moving.

After a while, Jann's back and thigh muscles ached from the constant pressure being put on them. She didn't know how much longer she could keep this up before starting to cramp. The descent was torturous. Finally Anika stopped moving, and whispered back at Jann, "I think we're here."

They waited.

The plan was that Alban and his colleague would go down to the main cavern via the stairs and spread the word. Then they would make their way to the access panel and open it. But it was still sealed shut. Down below, Jann could see Nills checking all around him, looking up and down. Maybe he had missed the opening.

He froze, then looked back at them and put his finger to his lips. He unshouldered the railgun and faced it towards the access panel. Jann could hear movement outside, then scraping on the duct walls. Finally light flooded in. Nills clambered out.

·   ·   ·

A FEW MINUTES later Jann was sitting on the floor beside a side wall of the main Colony Two cavern. It was an out of the way place, concealed at the front by a waist-high row of hydroponics. She rubbed some feeling back into her legs.

Alban had now been joined by several other betas. Fewer than Jann had hoped for, and with nothing useful as weapons. "Trouble," he said as they all crouched down.

"Define *trouble*," said Jann.

"Apparently they were expecting you... they thought you would arrive by the main entrance, so a heavily armed hybrid group are over there."

"Shit," said Nills. "How did they know we were coming? I thought Gizmo jammed the perimeter scanner?"

"Kayden," said Jann.

"Kayden?" Nills looked at her.

"Yes. Before we left Colony One, when I went off to say my goodbyes, he asked me how we were going to get in. I told him your crazy plan, you know... charge into the main entrance and start shooting."

Nills thought about this. "Why would Kayden tip off the hybrids? I mean, he's planning his exit off this rock."

"How else would they know?"

"But, say even if he wanted to, how would he make contact?"

"There must have been comms between the two facilities in the past. Maybe he got it working?"

"It doesn't make any sense."

"There's obviously something more going on than we can see yet, Nills."

A few more betas arrived. One knelt down and whispered to them. "Armed hybrids are moving out from the entrance."

"Shit, we don't have much time then." Nills poked his head over the row of vegetation, looked around and sat back down. "Okay, here's the plan. Over at the far end of the cavern is a wide stair leading up to the council chamber. We need to take that, and fast. Once we have it, Jann can rally the rest of the betas from the balcony overlooking the whole cavern. We'll go first, those with weapons directly behind, the rest of you spread the word. Any questions?"

They all looked petrified.

"Ready?"

"Let's do it," said Jann as she hefted a spear.

They crouched down and moved off, using the vegetation for cover. They zigzagged their way through the central cavern, extracting astonishment and shock from the betas they happened upon en route. Some simply stood back, but others merged in with the mob that was forming behind them.

Then it all went to rat shit.

From both left and right two pairs of hybrids appeared and started firing. Jann, Nills and Anika hit the deck, but the betas behind were not so fast. Three went down in the first volley, two more with the second, by the third they had all scattered into the dense vegetation.

Jann was pinned down behind a low grow-bed. Nills and Anika were a good five meters away, also unable to move. "Nills, cover me," she shouted. He nodded and started firing. Anika joined in. It was blind, no accuracy, it was just to draw the hybrids' fire.

She peeped out and gauged the distance to the nearest pair. She hefted her spear, stood up and threw it at them. It arrowed through the intervening space, skewered the left arm of the first one and embedded itself in the chest of the one directly behind. Jann dropped down again and looked over at Nills. He gave her the thumbs up, and started firing again. She joined in with the crossbow. Another hybrid was hit and went down. The fourth one decided not to hang around and backed off.

Behind her, the fallen were being dragged back to relative safety by their comrades. Some screamed in agony, others were dead. It was a mess. If she didn't do something now, they would lose all momentum. She stood up and raced over to them.

"Listen, you all know who I am. I've come back to help you find your way." Heads moved out from the undergrowth, she was connecting. "For too long you have lived in the dream world of your past, locked inside the memories of your alphas." She opened her arms to them. "But you are more than that, you are your own people, the first true Martians. This is your place, your home, your paradise. A heaven on Mars that you alone have built." More moved out from the undergrowth to listen. She continued, "There is no greater place here on this planet, not the surface dunes, not the great canyons, not even Colony One. This is your Eden, your birthright. It's time for you to take it back and claim it as your own."

By now a crowd had gathered and Jann could feel the mood changing. Their fear was subsiding, she could feel desire growing in them. She pressed on.

"We will storm the council chamber and hold Vanji to account for his actions. We take back what is yours, we do it now, and we do it quick." She raised a spear high above her head. "So who's with me?"

But before the crowd could react, two small canisters clanked and rolled across the floor, smoke hissing out from their sides. *Shit,* thought Jann, *Gas.* She reacted instantly and ran. But the betas weren't so fast. They began to cough and splutter and hold their throats as they scattered.

"Dammit." She had lost the moment. It was going against them. If she could not rouse them to action then there was no hope. She looked back up to the council chamber balcony. A hybrid was holding another gas canister, pulling a pin from the side, getting ready to throw it into the dispersing betas.

"Screw this." Jann judged the distance. It was a good forty meters; it was literally a long shot. She hefted a spear above her head and just when the hybrid was distracted with the pin mechanism, she fired. It shot through the space with impressive speed, arching slightly as it traversed the cavern. The hybrid looked up just in time to feel it bury itself in his skull, straight through his right eye. He tottered, one hand reached up as the other dropped the canister on the balcony floor. It rolled back into the council chamber as he fell.

A cheer went up from the betas. Jann seized her moment, turned around and raised another spear high in the air and shouted, "Who's with me?"

There was no mistaking the answer this time, a roar went up from the assembled crowd. She had them. A wild, enraged mob ready to do her bidding. She caught sight of Nills. He gave her the thumbs up again. "To the council chamber," she shouted and raced off across the cavern, the mob charging behind.

JANN, Nills and Anika led the way up the main stairway and into a broad hallway leading up to the council chamber. Already the effects of the gas were emptying the room. Hybrids staggered out, coughing and spluttering. But they were not going down without a fight. As Jann and Nills came out onto the central corridor they were met with a hail of fire. Nills yelled and clutched his right shoulder. He staggered backwards and fell back down the first few steps. They were forced back, behind the cover of the stairwell.

Nills grimaced in pain. "Bastards."

Jann grabbed the satchel of explosives that Nills was

carrying. She knelt down and rummaged through it. "Which are the flash bombs?" She held two up with different markings. He nodded to her left hand. "Are you sure?"

"No, I'm too busy dying here."

"Fuck it." Jann pulled the pin out and lobbed it down the hallway. A second or two later the whole space lit up with an incandescent flash. Smoke filled the corridor, screams echoed from the walls.

She turned back to the eager mob of betas crushing up the stairs behind them and raised her arms. "Quiet. Everybody. Stop where you are, wait." The mob murmured and muttered as they settled down. Jann shouted back down the hallway, "The next one's explosive. You saw what it did to the upper gallery, so don't make me throw one down on you."

The hallway was silent.

"The show is over, there's no way out, except through us. So lay down your weapons and surrender. You have ten seconds."

From far down the hallway Jann could hear voices arguing and debating. "Seven... six... five..."

"Okay, okay, we surrender."

A cheer rose up from the mob.

"Send the hybrid leader out first. Hold your weapon in the air, high above your head." Jann ventured a peek around the corner. Smoke and dust clouded the corridor and obscured her view, she could see very little.

Then, from out of the fog, a figure emerged. It was

Xenon, the hybrid leader, arms in the air, weapon over his head. Jann held up a grenade, pulled the pin, but held the lever tight. She moved towards him.

"Any sudden move and this gets lobbed into the council chamber."

Xenon moved slowly forward.

"That's close enough." A knot of betas had come up behind her. "Put the weapon on the ground slowly and step back. He did as she asked and she signaled to Anika to pick it up. Jann moved over to the entrance of the council chamber and shouted into the room.

"Everyone out of there now, weapons in the air."

The guards filed out first, then the three geneticists. They lined them up along the wall, kneeling on the floor. The room was emptied, save for Vanji. He was still inside.

NILLS HAD DECIDED he wasn't dying. He stood behind Jann, his right shoulder a bloody mess. "Vanji, Vanji." The mob had started chanting, baying for blood. It would be a lynching and Jann could do nothing to stop it.

"You've got to get them under control, Nills."

"Jann, you're the one they want to follow now. It's up to you."

"Listen, gather up a few betas you trust and put these guys under house arrest. Then we go in together and deal with Vanji. Okay?"

Nills went off and talked to Anika. As they were

putting a team together, Jann approached the hybrid leader. "The others, where are they?"

He did that same weird staring into space for a brief moment. "They have put down their weapons, they want a guarantee of safety."

"I can't guarantee that, but I will do my best." She turned to the betas and spoke in a loud, commanding voice.

"Listen up. The hybrids have surrendered along with the remains of the council. We have won, this colony is yours now. The fighting is over, I ask that no more blood be spilled."

"Vanji, we want Vanji."

Jann raised her hand. "Nills and I will deal with Vanji. Then we will let a new council of betas decide what to do." This seemed to placate the mob somewhat. She turned back to Anika. "Get a group down to the entrance cavern and disarm the rest of the hybrids. Put them under house arrest and let them stew for a while. No more killing... if you can manage it."

She nodded, and started to organize the mob into group. They seemed to respond well to her directions. Perhaps it was a symptom of the life they knew here. The safest option was to follow rather than lead.

Jann turned to Nills. "Okay, let's drag him out."

They entered the council chamber. It was empty.

"Dammit, he's not here?" Nills scanned the room.

Jann ran back out and grabbed Xenon by the shoulder. "Where is he? Where's he gone?"

"You're too late."

"What do you mean, too late?"

"He's left the planet."

For a moment Jann's world stood still as her brain tried to fathom this revelation. Slowly the wheels turned and she realized—she had been played all along.

"Kayden," she said.

The hybrid leader smiled. "Yes, Kayden."

"Shit," said Jann.

22

THE MAV

Jann stood over the hybrid leader in stunned silence. How could she have been so dumb as to give the launch codes to Kayden? She had never trusted him, she should have listened to her instincts. Too late now.

Nills slumped on the floor, gripping his badly injured arm. He was losing a lot of blood.

"Nills, shit. You need medical help." She called to some of the other betas, "Get him up, quick."

"I'm okay, there are others that need help more than me."

"You're not okay. You've got a three inch metal spike sticking out of your shoulder."

Two betas came over and helped him stand up. "Come on Nills, let's get to sickbay and get you patched up."

Nills groaned as he was lifted. "That bastard Vanji.

How did we not see this coming? He's going to get away with it."

"Maybe not," said Jann

"What do you mean?"

"What other vehicles are there in the entrance cavern? Anything working?"

"Possibly some quad-bikes. Why?"

"Because there may still be time. Depending on the orientation of the Odyssey in orbit, it can take several hours before launch."

"You mean they could still be on the surface?"

"Possibly. Listen, have someone bring my EVA suit to the entrance and get a mechanic to help me start one of those quad-bikes."

She started to move but Nills grabbed her arm. "You're not thinking of stopping them? That's crazy."

"Nills, do you really want him to get away with what he did here, all the recycling, all the torture?"

"No... but..."

"But nothing. Don't imagine for one minute that he's going back to Earth to put his feet up and retire. The knowledge he possesses has the potential to completely alter human society—and not for the better."

Nills' face melted into resignation.

"This was all planned, Nills. He's been working on this for a long time. Someone, or some group on Earth is helping him. That's the scary part. So he has to be stopped."

Nills nodded and then embraced her with his good

arm, in a tight grip. "I know. I just don't want you to go and die on us now."

Jann held his face in her hands and touched his forehead with her own. "It's not about us anymore. It's about humanity. It's about all that is right. You once said that to me... a long time ago."

She pulled away. "Just remember me." She ran off.

By THE TIME she got to the entrance cavern two betas were already working on one of the quad-bikes. Jann assumed it was one of these machines that Vanji must have used to make his escape. "Will it start?"

One poked his head out from the side of the bike. "Should do, give us some time." He stuck his head back into the guts of the machine. Two more betas rushed in carrying Jann's EVA suit and helmet. "We checked it over and it looks good for another three or so hours. After that you're out of power."

Jann nodded and stepped into the suit. *Well, here I go again,* she thought. *Back to saving the world. Not really what I had signed up to with the ISA.* She remembered her first few tentative steps on Mars after they landed. They weren't really steps, more like falling flat on her face. How things had changed since then.

The quad-bike burst into life, its engine's roar reverberating off the cavern walls. It cut out. "Crap." The mechanic poked at its innards and tried it again. It burst back to life. He revved the engine a few times.

"Okay, keep the revs high or it will cut out."

Jann nodded as she straddled the bike.

"If it does, then this button starts it, but it's a bit dicky. You've got about fifty klicks worth of fuel in it."

She revved the bike and popped the clutch. It jumped forward and cut out. She hit the start button a few times before it fired again.

"Open the airlock," she shouted at the mechanic as she released the clutch, slowly this time. The bike moved forward. "Okay," she said to no one in particular. "Let's do this." She closed her helmet visor and drove into the airlock.

THE QUAD-BIKE WAS FAST. Jann sped across the crater's surface leaving a wake of sand and dust billowing out behind her. It made short work of the distance and before long she could see the tip of the MAV in the distance. She twisted the throttle and the quad-bike picked up speed. She was bumped and jostled. Without the belt holding her on, she would have been tossed off several times already. But the thought of the MAV rising up from the planet's surface at any moment made her throw caution to the wind. She powered on. She was about eight hundred meters from the MAV when the bike cut out. "Shit." She tried to start it again, and again, and again. But no joy. "Shit, shit, shit." She banged on the handlebars. The MAV still stood motionless in the distance. There was nothing for it, she would have to run.

She moved with all the speed she could muster and closed the distance. She felt a sense of deja vu, remembering the last time she was out on the crater's surface trying to figure out how to stop Annis. But she had learned a thing or two since then. She and Gizmo had built the fuel tanks together, so Jann knew this time what to do to stop the MAV from launching. All she had to do was get there.

Gizmo entered her thoughts. Now would be a good time to have the little robot around. But it was buried under several tons of rock. *Poor Gizmo,* she thought. It had been a good friend to her, even when she was treating it like crap. What she wouldn't do to have it here with her now.

As she approached, Jann could see that all the fuel tanks were in position, so the countdown had probably begun. Disabling the MAV meant climbing up one of the landing struts to get access to the electronics that controlled the fuel flow. But if the MAV were to launch while she was attempting to get to it, she would be incinerated instantly.

Nevertheless, she started climbing and quickly located the panel. She popped the latch and exposed a sealed circuit board. She pulled it out and dropped back on to the surface. She had done it, Vanji was going nowhere.

Jann backed away from the base of the MAV, still clutching the circuit board. A little distance out she could see the rover that Kayden and the others had used, so she

GERALD M. KILBY

headed toward it. As she drew near she spotted two bodies on the ground. It was Noome and Samir. They had broken visors and both had a bloody hole in the middle of their forehead. They had been executed. They were not going back to Earth, it was never in the plan.

THE HATCH on the side of the MAV opened and a body emerged. It stopped on the top rung of the ladder when it saw Jann and stood for a moment, just looking at her. Jann's helmet comms crackled into life. "Malbec, eh... so you decided to come with us after all."

"Not exactly."

"So what are you doing here?" It was Kayden, she recognized the voice. He began to descend the ladder. Jann backed off.

"I assume Vanji is in there with you?"

"Why don't you come with us, back to Earth, back home? Think about it. You could see your family again."

"You mean like Noome and Samir. Was that the tale you spun for them?"

Kayden waved an arm. "We had a... dispute, you know how these things can go."

"They were never going home and neither was I. You just wanted the launch codes."

"That's not true, come..." he beckoned with his free arm. "Think about how pleased your family will be to see you."

"I don't have a family. My father died two years ago."

"I'm sorry to hear that, Jann. Really I am. But you have your ticket booked, so why not come with us off this rock?"

"It's over, Kayden. The betas control Colony Two now and they are baying for blood. So, no one's going anywhere. Especially not without this." She held up the circuit board up for him to see.

"Ah... I assume what you are holding is the reason our countdown has stopped?"

"Like I said, it's game over."

"Well, in that case, I too have something to show you." With that, he reached back in through the MAV hatch, and before Jann realized her mistake, it was too late.

Kayden retrieved a railgun and let rip with a long burst of fire. Jann turned to run but she was jolted forward by a blow to the back of the head. She stumbled and fell, grabbing her helmet with both hands. "Shit." How could she have been so stupid? He was playing her—again, keeping her talking, buying time.

She expected a stream of biometric alerts to flash up, but she got lucky, the railgun spike had not penetrated her helmet. She lifted her head up and looked over at the MAV. Kayden was reloading the gun. "Dammit." She had dropped the circuit board; it was still on the ground, undamaged. She needed to get to it before he did. But he was descending the ladder fast. He aimed again and fired another short burst. Several darts buried themselves in the ground just inches from her. She picked herself up and ran for a good distance before chancing a backward look.

Vanji had now left the MAV and was standing beside Kayden, examining the control board. Jann had stopped running, now that she was out of range of the railgun, and stood watching them. They seemed to be discussing what to do. Finally Vanji took the gun and Kayden headed off with the board, presumably to reinstall it—and there was nothing Jann could do about it. Vanji reloaded the gun and looked over at her. "I admire your tenacity, Dr. Malbec," his voice broke through on her helmet comms. "But it seems you have made your last play."

She could see Kayden climbing up the landing strut. "So what about the secrecy, the hiding out all these years?"

"You changed all that, Jann. When you showed up in the airlock in Colony Two."

"How so?" He was moving towards her.

"Your arrival allowed me to advance my plans."

"Like giving the colony over to the hybrids? That didn't work out too well."

"No matter, I had done all I could with Colony Two. Too many obstructionists, too many who were starting to get queasy about the direction we were taking."

"Like creating a new biologically reproductive species of human."

"That, and other plans. So it was time to leave. And you were the way home."

"Because I had the launch codes?" Jann was still backing away as Vanji advanced.

"Tell me, did you ever wonder why that clone showed up in the airlock in Colony One?"

She thought about this for a moment, it seemed a long time ago. She wasn't sure if she really cared.

"He was lonely?"

"I sent him. Well, more accurately I engineered it." Kayden was now back down on the surface and moving over to the ladder. The circuit board had been replaced, there was nothing to stop them leaving.

"Kayden discovered that Samir and Noome had been hacking ISA communication over the last few years. They had formulated a crazy plan to use this MAV to escape. But they needed the launch codes. So how to get you to come to us? Simple, Kayden helped them send one of the more demented betas, one who longed to visit the source of their creation."

"So you just played me the whole time."

"Yes, but to be fair, we had to gain your trust first."

"So the recycling, the escape plan, it was all a ruse?"

"Rather an effective one, don't you think?" Vanji glanced back over his shoulder to see Kayden re-enter the MAV.

"How do you know he's not going to leave you behind, Vanji?"

He fired off a burst but they went nowhere. But then

he bolted forward and fired again, darts peppered the ground around her. She turned to run but caught her boot on a rock and stumbled forward. Vanji sensed his chance and ran at her, firing as he went.

She felt a searing snap of pain course up her thigh as the first dart buried itself just above her right knee. The second spun her head around as it smashed off the side of her helmet. "No." She grabbed her leg to stop the air escaping. Vanji, seeing he had her now, stopped to reload. He cocked the gun and started towards her.

"Vanji, three minutes to launch, you'd better get back here now."

Vanji stopped for a moment. He was torn between finishing Jann off, and missing his flight to Earth. In the end, he turned on his heel and ran back to the MAV.

Jann watched him go as the air slowly escaped out of her EVA suit.

23

PALE BLUE LIGHT

D r. Jann Malbec dragged herself up from the dirt and balanced on one leg. Her heads-up display strobed alerts as her EVA suit tried hard to maintain pressure. She clamped a hand over her thigh, trying to slow the rate of evacuating air. A bolt of pain rifled up through her lower body. She could barely move.

There was no way she could make it back to the MAV, never mind try to prevent it from taking off. So she hobbled across the dusty Martian surface, as fast as the pain in her leg would allow, towards the abandoned rover. All the time the heads up display flashed warnings with ever more urgency until she finally crawled into the rover airlock and pressurized it. She popped opened her helmet visor and collapsed onto the cockpit seat.

Through the window she could see the Mars ascent vehicle, ticking down the seconds until lift off—and there was nothing she could do. Rage welled up inside her. They had played her for a fool, strung her along, and she had fallen for it. She willingly handed over the launch codes and doomed humanity to a future of genetic tyranny. As she sat and waited for the inevitable, a new sense of loss began to compound her anger. Now that the time had come for the MAV to perform its function, return its occupants to the orbiter, and ultimately to Earth, she realized that her last hope of going home would be leaving with it. She thought she had reconciled herself to this fate when she agreed to return to Colony Two with Nills, but now that she was face to face with it, the feeling of abandonment cut her deep.

Over the years, she had clung to the fragile hope that someday, she would be able to return to Earth. But that dream would soon be gone, perhaps forever. She was being robbed of her hope, her dream, it was being taken away from her and there wasn't a damn thing she could do about it. She could only watch. The MAV started venting gas, prepping the engines for ignition. Her anger intensified.

"Well, if I can't have it, then nether will you, Vanji." She stood up and hobbled to the EVA suit storage area at the back of the rover. From an overhead locker she frantically pulled out a container of suit repair patches and applied several to her leg, as she sat back in the cockpit seat. She flipped her visor closed. The heads up display showed the patches were holding. She had around twenty minutes of air remaining. *Should be enough,* she thought.

Jann started the engine, it rumbled into life. Then she hit the comms and spoke. "Vanji?" There was a hiss of static before a response broke into to the helmet.

"Dr. Malbec, your power of survival is impressive."

"There's just one last thing before you go."

"What's that?"

"Go screw yourself." With that, Jann pointed the rover at the MAV and rammed the throttle fully forward. She stuck a few patches over it to lock it into position and ran to the rear airlock. With just seconds to spare she jumped out of the back of the speeding rover onto the surface. She hit the ground hard and fast, and rolled several times before finally coming to rest. She had just enough time to look around and see the rover speed toward the MAV.

At first she thought it was going to miss, but it caught the edge of one of the landing struts. Then everything happened all at once. The MAV began to topple just as the engines ignited, and there was a split second when she thought it might actually lift off. But it didn't. Instead it exploded in a gigantic fireball.

Even in the thin Martian atmosphere, the force felt like a kick to her chest. Dust billowed out from the epicenter and debris rained down, peppering the ground all around her. She rolled face down and covered her head with her hands. It was a reflex action and would do nothing to protect her if she was hit by any fragment of the MAV. Something struck the ground inches from her head, then something else. She had to move, get out of the zone, fast. She picked herself up and hobbled as best she could. She wasn't sure of the direction as the atmosphere was immersed in sand and dust. New alerts flashed on her heads up, the suit was losing pressure. "Shit." Either the patches weren't holding or she had torn it again. She kept going.

After a few minutes the air began to clear and she sat down for a moment to gather her strength. The pain in her leg came back with a vengeance. She was breathing hard, using up valuable air she didn't have to spare. "Calm down, focus," she said to herself. "You can still do this."

Her plan had been to patch the suit enough to make the walk back to Colony One. It wasn't that far. But now she wasn't so sure. It was losing pressure and worked hard to backfill with nitrogen reserves. Ordinarily this would be fine but she was low on resources. Her display calculated she had around ten minutes left. She had better get going. Jann stood up again and looked back at where the MAV had been. All she could see was an enormous cloud of dust. Probably nothing remained of it but a charred hulk of metal. It was gone, along with Vanji and Kayden, and any chance she ever had of leaving Mars. "Move." She forced herself to start walking.

THE FASTER SHE moved the more oxygen she would use up, the slower she went the less chance she would have to make it to Colony One in time. "Don't think about it, just keep moving." She could see its massive dome off in the distance. *Home,* she thought. It really did feel like that to her. She had spent so many years there it was part of her, it was what defined her. It kept her moving forward, beckoning to her, calling out her name like a loving parent standing in the doorway with open arms, welcoming you back after a long journey away. She kept going.

Her suit was running dangerously low on oxygen, she could feel it, her steps were getting shorter, more labored as her body grew progressively weaker from hypoxia. Her mind was getting fuzzy, her thoughts muddled.

Why had she done it? Killed Vanji. She could have let him go and taken the rover back to Colony One. She would not be in this position now. Was it out of some grand moral outrage she felt for what this technology would do to the socioeconomics of Earth? What did she care what happened to Earth. Or was it simply her rage? Rage for what Vanji did to her, rage for her time in the horror of the recycling tank? But did it go deeper than that? Rage for being abandoned by the ISA, by Earth, by all that she had known and loved. Rage for the loss of Paolio and Nills and all her friends, all gone, all dead. She stopped, and slumped down on to ground on her knees. She looked up at the dome of Colony One, so near, so far.

Yes, she had been abandoned by them all, and now it seemed even Mars was letting her go. It had no more left to give her. Jann sat back on her heels, she too had no more left to give. She had five minutes remaining and for most of that she would probably be unconscious. She might as well make the best of it.

Jann looked up at the sky. It was a beautiful evening. Over the crater rim to the west the sun was sinking below the horizon, bathing the sky in a pale blue and purple light. Out across the crater plateau she could see a dust devil swirl and twist its way towards her. She watched it for a time, mesmerized by its dance. Mars hadn't abandoned her after all. It was showing her its best, giving her a final sendoff.

She collapsed down on her back and stared up at the heavens. It was growing darker as her life was ebbing away. A dust cloud blew up around her as she took a deep breath, exhaled very slowly, and finally closed her eyes.

24

SEARCH

The hybrids had been disarmed and were now corralled in a number of secure areas throughout Colony Two. They had split them up into several smaller groups, the eighteen that were left. But was this secure enough? The species possessed a strange telepathic ability, so even dividing them up was probably pointless in preventing them from communicating. Nills knew they would ultimately have to find some way for them to regain the trust of the betas, and vice-versa. They were still a problem, but for the moment, at least they were not a threat. As for the remaining geneticists, their future looked increasingly tenuous. Now that the betas were in control, some were getting drunk on power and were stoking up the mob to seek revenge. Like all great upheavals, the aftermath can be as chaotic, if not more so, than the event itself.

As Nills sat in sickbay, surrounded by the dead and the dying from the battle, he realized that the situation could get out of control very quickly. There was a distinct possibility that a cohort of the betas could turn into a rage-fueled mob, and start to agitate for retribution for the loss of their friends and loved ones. The geneticists would be first, then the hybrids, then... where would it go? Anyone who stood in their way?

It was at that very moment Nills realized that they were indeed, truly human. They might be clones, they might have been subservient, but scratch the surface and, underneath it all, they still possessed the same violent instincts. All it needed was the spark, and the ugly side of humanity would ignite.

It didn't help that Jann had gone. If she were here she could have exerted a level of control. None of them would go against her wishes, seeing her as almost divine. But she had left, and as the hours passed, Nills wondered if she would ever return.

"I say recycle them, they deserve it." Alban was agitating.

"Yeah, a quick death's too good for them." Others were shouting out now.

"Let's take them down to the tanks and throw them in."

"No. We will do nothing until Dr. Malbec returns."

Nills raised his voice so that all the betas that had assembled around him in sickbay could hear. They mumbled and grumbled. He might be injured but he was still their leader and the mere mention of Jann's name still held some authority. "They're no threat to us at the moment, so keep them locked up, and keep a close eye on them."

They grumbled some more but it seemed to have quelled the dissent—for the moment. Nills knew he had very little time to try and keep a lid on things. He surveyed the group around him; he knew them all by name. They looked at him intently waiting for leadership. A great weight of responsibility had been thrust upon him, made even greater by the fact that Vanji had killed most of the natural leaders in the colony. There was really only him now, and Jann, but she might well be dead. All he had was the authority to use her name. Would that be enough?

He was no politician either, he was an engineer, he thought in straight lines, in cause and effect, action and reaction, working the problem. So, the first thing he needed to do was to get them busy and get them distracted.

"Before we do anything, we need a full assessment of the damage. I want each of you responsible for your sectors to give me a full report on the state of our resources. You all know the importance of life support. We don't need some system going off the rails now or we

GERALD M. KILBY

all die, and that will be the end of everything. So get to it and I want shift supervisors to report back to me in... three hours. Got it?"

They grumbled a little more but when you spend your entire life depending on the maintenance of artificial life support you learn to respect it. It becomes top priority. Nills knew this would focus their minds. Any thought of a systems failure would kick them into action. So they dispersed, one by one, to their appointed sectors.

Anika and Alban remained.

"Why don't you just let them have their way with the goddamn geneticists?" Alban kept his voice low so the others in sickbay would not hear.

"Do you know what would happen to us if they were to die?"

"We would be rid of them, that's what."

"Yes, we would. And we would all die because of it."

Alban didn't reply, he just gave a quizzical look. He didn't understand.

Nills stood up from the edge of the bed and tested his arm. It hurt like hell but he felt a little better. The shock had worn off and his body was coming to terms with the new normal. He moved it around to test the extent of the pain; it was manageable.

"Genetic engineering is the reason that this colony can exist. If it wasn't for all the synthetic microbes in here there would be no clean air, no soil to grow food, no way

198

to recycle waste, no resource processing... do you want me to go on?"

Alban sighed. "Yeah, I know. Just saying, that's all."

"Much as I hate the bastards, we really need them. Without them we will all die. Maybe not right away, it would take time, but as soon as some problem occurred we would not have the knowledge to solve it. It would be like a spaceship without a pilot, a reactor without an engineer."

"We need to keep them safe," said Anika. "Not let them be recycled."

"What about throwing them a hybrid or two?"

"Alban, no one is getting recycled, okay?"

"Just a thought."

"Look I really need you guys with me on this. Justice will be done, but only when things settle down and we have some control of the situation. If we start now then where does it end? Will they then want to recycle Rachel and Becky?"

"Wait a minute. Has anybody seen them?" said Anika.

They looked at each other. Nobody had. They were now the last two original colonists, excluding the geneticists. They were like Noome and Samir, always kept a low profile, avoided the attentions of the council. They wanted no part of Vanji's world. They just wanted a quiet life. But they were alphas, and as such could be a potential target for mob.

"Shit, no. You don't think they're in trouble?"

"Alban, pull some of your people off guard duty and

go find them. They have no part in this, I don't want to see them hurt."

"Okay." But he didn't seem too enthusiastic.

"And don't forget they were an endangered species, too. Vanji had it in for any alpha that didn't see things his way. He rid himself of most of them over the years, so don't let anything happen to them on our watch. Find them."

"I'll try." Alban headed out of the sickbay.

"Anika, how are you with EVA?" It seemed like a simple question but betas did not go outside and had no experience in an EVA suit. It was a dangerous business without training, as you never knew how someone would react. They could quite easily freak out. Putting someone in an EVA suit with no training, and shoving them out an airlock could be disastrous. Even Nills had a tough time when they were all entering Colony Two from the rover. And he knew Lars was barely keeping it together. But, Anika... she seemed like a natural, very composed. It was her nature.

"What have you got in mind?"

He looked around, held her gently by the elbow and led her out of sickbay into the empty corridor beyond. "I may have made a mistake."

"Mistake? What do you mean?"

"Because I said we do nothing until Jann returns. I've just bought us some time, nothing more. The longer she stays away, the harder it will be to keep control. Then things might come to a head."

"You mean if she doesn't return?"

"Exactly. And, let's face it, that doesn't look likely to happen. She should be back by now, there was only around three hours life support in her suit."

Anika didn't reply; the reality of the situation was only just dawning on her.

"We need to find her, even if it's just bringing back the body," whispered Nills.

"Shit, you really think she is dead?"

"I really don't know."

"So, what do you want me to do?"

"Go and get the rover back into the colony. Have them check it over and refuel it. Then we go searching for her."

"Okay."

"Come on, I'll walk with you down to the main entrance cavern. I need the betas to see me up and moving, I need to look like I know what I'm doing."

OVER THE NEXT hour Nills set up command in the entrance cavern. Anika had retrieved the rover and it was now being given the once over by the mechanics, by betas that Nills knew well, engineers like himself. Alban had also managed to find the last of the alphas, Rachel and Becky. They had been hiding out where they always hid out. They were not the brightest pair in the colony, but to be fair, they were smart enough to be two of the few original colonists left alive, Nills gave them that. They sat now in the cavern, under Nills' protection. They looked shit scared. Part of him felt sorry for them.

"Do either of you guys remember how to use an EVA suit?"

Neither of them answered, they just looked even more scared. They really didn't know what was happening. Maybe they thought Nills was about to do a *lockout* on them. It was a phrase used to describe when someone was shoved into an airlock with no suit, and the outer door opened.

"Look," Nills stood up and came over to them. "We need some help. Betas don't EVA, at least not very well, and most of them have never seen the planet's surface up close. But you guys have."

Becky nodded. "It's been a while, you know... a few years."

"That's better than never. We need to find Dr. Malbec. That means taking the rover and looking. We may need to EVA and search around. You think you could help me?"

Rachel's eyes were like saucers. "You mean actually go outside?"

"Yes, out there." Nills pointed at the airlock.

They looked at one another, then Becky said, "I would do anything to get back out onto the surface, see the sky again, anything."

"I'll take that as a *yes* then?"

"I'm with her, make that two."

"Good." Nills turned around to one of the

maintenance crew. "Check through those suits and get me two more fully resourced."

"I'll see what I can do."

"How much longer before the rover is ready?"

"Half an hour, give or take."

"Okay." Nills shouted across the cavern to Anika. She was helping with the rover servicing so had her head buried in its engine bay. "Anika." She popped her head out. He signaled to her to follow him and walked over to a quiet spot out of earshot of the others. She followed him over, wiping her hands on an oily rag as she went.

"Anika, I want you to stay here, help Alban keep things under control."

"What? No, you can't do this on your own, Nills."

"I'm taking the two alphas, they can EVA, they've been outside, they have the experience."

"Those two," she nodded over to where the two alphas were sitting. "You can't be serious."

"Listen, they may look like a pair of dopes but they have way more experience out on the surface than anyone else here. And if I leave them here, god knows what will happen to them. End up in a tank, maybe."

Anika screwed her mouth up. "Hmmm, I suppose."

"Anyway, I need you here to help keep the betas from doing something stupid."

"You stay, Nills. They respect you more. Let me go and find Dr. Malbec."

"No, this is something I've got to do. I need to know for sure."

"Okay, but be careful. If we lose you as well..." she placed a gentle hand on his elbow. "We'll really be up shit creek."

The sound of the rover engine starting up reverberated in the cavern and they looked over. The mechanic gave them the thumbs up. Nills nodded back, then looked over to where Rachel and Becky were getting ready. One was holding an EVA suit, looking it up and down like she was trying to work out how to get in to it. *This is not filling me with a lot of confidence*, thought Nills.

So it was that when the rover finally rumbled out of the airlock, Nills felt a deep uneasiness about what he was doing. How much was he putting the stability of Colony Two and all that they had fought for in jeopardy by leaving? The situation was still volatile. Now that blood had been tasted, there was a faction within the betas that wanted more.

He didn't have to do this. Anika could have done the search. What's more, Jann knew the risks when she charged off to stop Vanji, it was reckless of her. What did she have to gain? If it had been up to Nills, he would have let him go. Good riddance to him—and to Earth. But with Jann he suspected it was personal, perhaps she had a deeper connection to the planet they had all left. In truth, none of the betas had ever seen Earth and they were more a part of this planet, this was their home. What did they care for a long forgotten world?

It didn't take long before they could see a tall plume of dust rising high into the atmosphere. Rachel checked the map on the rover main navigation screen. "Looks like that's coming up from the ISA MAV location."

"You think they launched, is that a vapor trail?"

"I'm not sure, we never got to see a takeoff. Remember we came here to stay. There was no going back for any of us."

It seemed to Nills to take forever to close the distance to the location. But as the rover drew closer, they began to make out the charred remains of the MAV revealing itself from within the cloud of dust that shrouded the site. All around lay a thick carpet of crumpled metal and debris.

"It must have been some explosion. What a mess," said Rachel as she brought the rover to stop, several meters away from the charred hulk.

"I think it's safe to say they didn't take off."

"No one could have survived that." Becky looked at Nills.

He surveyed the devastation. "If Jann was caught up in that explosion then I think we're looking for a body. Okay, let's get out and take a look."

Rachel and Becky flipped down their visors and checked each other's EVA suits with a practiced, confident efficiency. Perhaps Nills had figured them wrong. In Colony Two they had come across as a pair of slackers, avoiding anything that looked like work. But now he was beginning to realize that this might have been just an act. The best way for them to stay alive was to not be noticed by Vanji. Maybe they were a lot smarter than he had initially given them credit for.

They cleared the airlock and started scouring the site for bodies, and it wasn't long before Nills found one. His heart skipped a beat when he spotted a pair of legs sticking out from under a mound of wreckage. He tapped his helmet comms. "Over here, give me a hand."

They lifted off a blackened wedge of fuel tank casing to reveal two bodies. "Samir." Nills said as he knelt down to inspect the broken visor. "And Noome," said Becky. "Looks like they were killed. See the wounds on their foreheads? They were never going to leave, were they?"

"No. They were just pawns, a means to an end, nothing more." Nills stood up, saddened at all the carnage that had taken place, but relieved it wasn't Jann that they had found. They widened their search.

"Nills, over here. What do you make of this?" Rachel's voice broke in to Nills' helmet, he looked up so see her bending down examining a patch of ground, far away from the epicenter of the explosion.

There was a lot of disturbance. The sand had been trampled and shifted from its natural state. A set of parallel caterpillar tracks led into the spot where the three of them now stood.

"What sort of machine would make tracks like that?" Rachel pointed off along the lines. "Looks like they came from the direction of the colony." She bent down to examine them more closely.

"It's not a rover or a quad-bike."

"I know of only one thing on this planet that could make tracks like that," said Nills.

"What's that?"

"Gizmo."

25

DUST DEVIL

When the initial shock wave from the detonation hit Gizmo's sensors, it did exactly the same thing that any human would have done—it ran like hell. The difference, of course, was the little droid's ability to analyze and compute at speeds a human could not even comprehend. In a fraction of a nanosecond it had calculated speed, force and acceleration of the impending shockwave. It then extrapolated, from the multitude of possible options it had, the best direction to run. Or, in this case, the least worst direction to take. So as the first rocks were being torn from the gallery roof Gizmo had decided to move back down the entrance tunnel—at full speed. This was still not enough for it to escape the impact completely. The explosion hit the little robot with sufficient force to knock it over and send it tumbling down the tunnel for at least twenty-five meters. Gizmo's systems went into the robotic equivalent of a nervous breakdown. Energy spiked, sensors overloaded, circuits fused and data corrupted.

It finally came to rest halfway down the tunnel, flat on its back. Even for Gizmo's speed of thought it took quite a while to reassemble its brain function and figure out the extent of the damage. The first thing it did was assess the state of its systems. Several sensor inputs were gone: infrared, ultra-violet, radiation. It still had ultrasonics so it could still determine range and proximity. Its radio antennas were history so no comms, and no way to connect with the broader data environment of Colony Two, or anywhere else for that matter. But its tracks were intact so it could move. Its power source was also intact. However, one of its arms had suffered severe damage and was not responding to any signals, it was still attached, but totally dead. After it made a full inventory of its remaining capabilities Gizmo turned its attention to— what to do?

The little droid analyzed the situation. Jann, Nills and the betas were on the other side of several tons of rock, assuming they were still alive. Gizmo put that at an approximate 56.4% probability. It could try and dig its way out. But it did not have enough power to complete the task. So it eliminated that as an option. Another option was to simply put itself into sleep mode and wait it out. Someone would find it eventually. It seemed like a reasonable choice but it was the least productive.

However, it could still get back out on to the surface,

through the entrance airlock at the far end of the tunnel. And then what? Try and get back into Colony Two by some other route? Or, it could simply return to Colony One. It was a long journey for the little robot, and it would take a few hours, but it would have just enough power to complete it. There was much to do back in the colony, and it was being left unattended and maintenance tasks would only increase the longer it was left idle. Gizmo made its decision. Of the three options open to it, returning to Colony One was the most productive. It powered up its tracks and sped off down the tunnel.

Once out on the surface of the crater basin Gizmo adjusted its speed to maximize power consumption. If it went too fast it would use too much power and not make it, too slow and its other systems would consume more energy than necessary. So it moved across the crater at a leisurely pace—for a robot. But even at this speed, its tracked wheels kicked up a tall tail of dust high into the Martian sky. It looked like a dust devil dancing across the plateau.

It had taken well over an hour to traverse most of the area, and it was nearing Colony One when its ultrasonics detected an atmospheric disturbance. A waveform of an amplitude compatible with an explosion entered its silicon consciousness. Gizmo searched its internal map of the crater to ascertain where it might have emanated from. The only thing it had was the location of the ISA ascent vehicle. Gizmo stopped. This new data required further analysis. It had estimated it would still have approximately 7.63% power remaining when it finally entered the airlock at Colony One. To detour via the source of the explosion would use up a further 2.7%. This was within limits, so the little robot altered direction and headed for the site of the MAV.

From a distance Gizmo could detect the dust cloud surrounding the site. And even with its limited sensory input it ascertained that not much was left of the launch craft. As it moved closer Gizmo bounced ultrasonics off the burnt out husk. It determined that the rover was the most likely initiator of the destruction. Someone must have crashed it into the MAV. Gizmo scanned the area looking for more data to work with, its power was running low so it hadn't much time to waste. It found nothing to warrant any further investigation. Whatever happened was over, time to move on, nothing to see here. So it turned and made for Colony One.

At around seven hundred meters from epicenter, Gizmo's sensors picked up a new object, a body shaped form, lying on the ground. The robot moved as fast as its power mode would allow and stopped at the site of the prostrate form. It would have liked to access the Colony One systems and get some data from the EVA suit's bio-monitor. But Gizmo's antenna array was long gone so it couldn't tell if the person was still alive or not. With its one functioning camera it scanned the face behind the visor. It was Dr. Jann Malbec.

"Well now, Jann," it said to itself. "You do seem to be in a spot of bother."

Gizmo could not lift her with just one arm, but it could drag her. But there were two problems with this. One, it would be risking damaging her suit, and killing her for certain if it ripped it enough to lose pressure. And two, it would be draining power fast with the added energy requirements of hauling a body.

But, it was here to assist, that was the little robot's motto, so assist it would. Gizmo reached down, clamped a metal hand onto the shoulder strap of Jann's EVA suit and started dragging her towards the airlock.

Power drained at an alarming rate. Worse, it was slowing down, too much torque was needed. It realigned its circuits and shut down all but its most essential systems. It kept moving, inching its way slowly to the airlock door.

The final power requirements needed to drag Dr. Jann Malbec up the ramp and into the airlock were virtually all that Gizmo had to give. The outer door closed and it sensed the airlock pressurizing. Then, with the very last few milliamps of its resources it reached down and popped open her helmet visor. It was all the little robot was able to do. It had done what it could, it had no more left to give.

26

SCHISM

"Gizmo?"

Nills looked up and smiled. "Yeah, it's a robot, it must have survived the rock fall."

"A robot?"

Nills waved a hand. "It's a long story, I'll explain it to you some other time." He stood up and examined the site. "See here," he pointed. "It came to this area, moved around quite a bit, and then headed off in that direction." He stood up and pointed off in the distance.

"The tracks look very different though, like it was dragging something behind it." He bent down again. "See the way there's a deep trough gouged out of the sand? Must have been something heavy."

"A body?"

Nills stood. "Maybe. Let's take the rover and follow it. Come on."

It didn't take Nills long before he realized the tracks

were heading for Colony One. When they arrived at the facility, they parked the rover and followed the tracks on foot, right up to the main entrance airlock. As Nills pushed the button to open the outer door, he did so with a deep sense of trepidation. Was it Jann's body that Gizmo was dragging?

It took a few moments for the airlock to pressurize and the inner door to open. Gizmo was standing in the airlock. It waved a metal hand. "Greetings, Earthlings."

"Gizmo, you're alive," said Nills as he popped open his visor.

"Technically no, since I am a robot. But I am operational. Well mostly." It tried to move its damaged arm, which just made a low grinding noise.

"Where's Jann?" Nills had his helmet off.

"You will be glad to hear that she is alive and well, and in the biodome." It raised its good arm towards the connecting entrance.

Nills got the EVA suit off in seconds and ran through the tunnel, past the rows of hydroponics and out on to the central dais, just as Jann was stepping out of the pond.

"Jann."

She looked up and smiled. "Nills, what took you so long?"

THEY SAT for a while on the central dais and talked. The little robot had saved her skin, for the second time. It was becoming a habit. Jann had woken to find herself in the Colony One airlock. She crawled her way to the medlab, patched herself up, and, when she managed to regain some strength, dragged Gizmo off to its recharging station. But she had no way to communicate with Colony Two, to let Nills know she was still alive. Even though Kayden had had some way to do it, she couldn't find it. Also, she had no transport. One rover was in Colony Two and the other was a charred metal husk. She had considered trying to drag back the quad-bike but now that was not necessary. Nills had come.

He filled her in on all that had happened as Rachel and Becky spent their time wandering around the facility, simply remembering things. Looking at this and that and sharing stories of times past. Nills had forgotten that they had lived here for quite some time. Perhaps they thought they would never see it again.

After a time Nills decided he needed to report back to Anika and let her know they were all okay. He took his leave, donned his EVA suit again and headed out to the rover to use the comms. As he sat down in the rover cockpit Nills gave a satisfied sigh, things had worked out. Jann was alive and some sense of control could now be established. He flipped the comms unit on. "Colony Two, this is Nills, over."

Static filled the rover. He tried again. "Colony Two, this is Nills, are you hearing me?"

"Nills, where are you?" It was a voice Nills didn't recognize.

"At Colony One, We found Jann, she's fine."

"That's great, but you better get your ass back here as quick as you can."

"Why, what's going on?"

"It's Alban. He and a few others have taken the geneticists and Xenon down to the tanks. I think they're going to recycle them. We can't do anything to stop it, you need to get back here... like now."

"Oh shit," said Nills.

JANN COULD TELL something was wrong by the look on Nills' face when he returned.

"We've got to get back, now... this minute."

"Why, what's going on?"

"Alban. I warned him not to do it, explained all the reasons, I thought he understood."

"What, Nills... do what?"

Nills stopped for a moment. "They're going to tank the geneticists... and the hybrid leader. If they do, then all that knowledge will be lost to us. I explained to him the reasons why we need them, but he is just blinded by hate and revenge."

"Shit."

NILLS WANTED the alphas to come back with him but Jann intervened. A leader he might be but the subtleties of politics were lost on him.

"They have to stay here," she argued.

"But why? They're on the same side as us, they could be useful."

"No offense, guys," she turned to them, and opened her hands out for emphasis, "But you're alphas. Your presence with us will only confuse the loyalties of those we need to rally."

They both gave a look of relieved acceptance.

"Also, I doubt you'd be much good in a fight."

They stood silent, like two school kids being chastised. But they were no fools either, they had not survived this long by sticking their necks out.

"That's settled, you stay here and try not to break anything. Gizmo, keep an eye on them."

"Certainly, Dr. Malbec."

27

XENON

Jann pushed the rover hard. It bounced and rocked as it sped across the expanse of the Jezero Crater basin. Nills had managed to contact Anika. The situation was delicate, but had not deteriorated—yet.

Alban and a small group of betas, those who had argued most for retribution, had seized their chance while Nills had gone to look for Jann. With her presumed dead, a momentary power vacuum had opened up and they rushed in to fill it. It was a wild sort of counter rebellion, it was mob rule.

They had argued with the betas holding the captives and demanded they be handed over. Anika had tried to talk them down but she wasn't getting any support. So, rather than see beta fighting beta, she had to back down.

Then followed a period of confusion as they debated what they would do to them, now that they had the upper hand. In the end they had taken all of the remaining geneticists and Xenon, the hybrid leader, down to the tanks. They would be made to pay the price. Justice would be served.

But they had not thought it through. It was not a quick death, not a hanging or death by firing squad. The counterrevolutionaries had barricaded themselves in the birthing room hoping to wait it out. Waiting for the point after which the body may be technically alive, but incapable of sustaining life outside the tank. How long was this? No one was really sure, but it was several hours at least. Although it would still take a few weeks to fully dissolve a live human in the tank.

When the rover finally lumbered into the main entrance airlock in Colony Two, quite a few betas had assembled there to greet them. Word of their return had spread. As Jann stepped out and removed her helmet she could sense the feeling of adulation that emanated from the group. It was something that didn't sit easy with her, too much responsibility, perhaps. It was a dangerous thing, one false word, or some casual action on her part could have unintended repercussions.

"What's the situation now?" Nills directed his question at Anika who had been trying to hold the line in his absence.

"They have them down in the birthing room, the

doors are all locked and barricaded from the inside, there's no way in."

"Well, they're not going anywhere soon. It takes a long time to die in the tank, so we've got some time." Jann had removed her EVA suit.

Nills walked over to a workbench and stood up on it so he could see over the assembled betas. "Listen up. We're going to break our way in to the birthing room and we are going to rescue those people."

"Let them die," someone shouted.

"Okay. And when they're finished with them, they'll come for the rest of the hybrids. After that, they'll come for the last of the alphas. And after that, they come for you." Nills jabbed a finger at the crowd. "So tell me, who will be left to save you when that happens?"

There was muted chorus of mumbling from the crowd.

"That's right—no one. Because you will have stood by and let them all be killed. This is not what we fought for, this is not who we are. So let's get these people out of there." He jumped down from the workbench. It had done the trick. The mood had shifted, their confidence was returning. Jann had to hand it to him. The old Nills would have been proud.

THE PLAN WAS SIMPLE. Break open the main door into the labs with a laser cutter, then start removing the barricade. After that it was talk. If that failed, then they would figure something out. Anika had organized a cutting crew, Nills was busy recruiting and arming some of the more levelheaded betas. Jann chose instead to visit the remaining hybrids, to assure them they were safe and that attempts were being made to rescue their leader, unharmed.

She made her way to the operations room next to the council chamber, on the upper level of the main cavern. Unlike the chamber itself this had not sustained any damage from the earlier fight to overthrow Vanji. It was from this room the council kept an eye on all activity within the colony. Around the walls were mounted dozens of monitors, all made with the same organic material as the ceiling illumination. They had a strange eerie look to them as they had no discernible edge, just patches of video here and there. She studied the feeds from the holding rooms for a few minutes.

"What are they doing?"

"I don't know," said one of the technicians. "They were fine up until thirty minutes ago... you know, walking, talking, that sort of thing. Now this." He waved a hand at the screen.

The hybrids were all huddled on the floor in groups, groaning and moaning. Holding their heads, eyes filled with sheer terror.

"Christ." Jann stepped back in horror. "It's their hive-mind. What one feels they all feel."

The technician looked intently at the screen. "I still don't get what's wrong with them."

"Alban has just tanked Xenon. They are feeling what he's feeling. What it's like to slowly dissolve to death."

The technician stood speechless, his mouth wide open.

"Do you have a feed from the labs?"

"No, all cameras are cut. But that one there is from the corridor." He pointed to a feed of the crew that was trying to cut open the main lab door. *Shit,* thought Jann, *they're going too slow.* She raced out of the operations room and headed to the labs. She found Nills resting against the wall of the corridor, just down from where the crew was working. He was armed to the teeth, along with Anika and two others. He wasn't taking any chances. The crew had finished opening the door and were now removing the equipment used to block the entrance.

"Nills," Jann shouted. He smiled when he saw her coming. "Xenon has already been tanked."

"How do you know?"

She explained what she had seen. "So we have to get him out of the tank quick, before he's passed the point of no return. The point where his body cannot sustain life outside the tank. If we don't hurry then we'll doom the remaining hybrids to weeks of writhing agony—it may even kill them all."

"Dammit," was the best reply Nills could manage.

"Nills," one of the crew shouted up to him. "We're nearly through."

"Okay." Nills signaled to his team and they moved up to the lab entrance, taking up positions either side of the doorway. It had been fully cleared. Nills stuck his head around the doorjamb.

"Alban, this is Nills here. Killing those captives will do us no good. We need them to survive. Nobody else has the knowledge."

There was a moment of silence. Nills moved in through the door. The others followed, keeping low. Once inside they spread out across the space of the vast lab cavern. They could see Alban and a few others at the far end, standing beside one of the birthing tanks.

"Alban." Nills held his hand up in the air. "Give it up. This is pointless."

Alban swung around, reached for a railgun and pointed it at him. Nills kept his hands high and moved forward, slowly.

"That's far enough. Come any closer and I will shoot you." He looked like he meant it.

"Where are the geneticists?" Nills stopped. Jann had slipped off to the side and was moving closer, using the tanks as cover.

"They're getting what they deserve. Except now that you've showed up we'll need to speed up the process." He shouted back to the others who were now all pointing weapons. "Bring them out, we'll do it here."

Two geneticists were dragged out from behind one of the tanks. Their hands were tied behind their backs and they both had defeated looks on their faces. They were forced down on their knees in front of Alban.

"This is for our friends." He pointed the railgun at

one of the forlorn figures and fired. A spray of blood exploded from the back of his skull, he collapsed backwards, and everyone lost it—fire erupted from both sides.

Nills dove for cover, metal barbs bouncing off the floor as he ran. One of Alban's crew went down. There was a scream from one of the betas. Jann hit the deck just as the tank behind her got hit and exploded into a thousand glass shards. The contents spilled out in a deluge, and with it came a body with tubes and wires still connected— it was Xenon, the Hybrid leader.

The ooze spread out across the floor in all directions and sloshed around Jann's feet as she peered around the edge of a tank she was using as cover. The hybrid kicked and squirmed. Several other bodies lay on the floor, dead. But there was no sign of Alban. So Jann crawled out from behind the tank toward the writhing body of the hybrid. Nills appeared on the other side.

"Nills," she called. "We need to get those tubes out of him quick."

Nills nodded and looked behind him to see Anika and a few others moving forward. He signaled for them to take up covering positions.

Jann rushed over to Xenon. "Nills, hold him down, stop him moving."

Nills grappled with the squirming body. "Dammit, he's really slippery."

Jann cut away the wires that had entangled him and

pulled out the long tube running down his throat. He coughed, and spluttered, and spat. Then he started to shiver violently. Nills released his grip. "Shit, he's going into shock."

"He'll be okay. Remember I've been here, I survived. But we do need to get him to sickbay."

Nills called over to the betas that were now coming into the lab. They had been drawn in by the unfolding drama, but were keeping their distance all the same.

"Hey, over here. Get him to sickbay." A few ran forward, gathered him up and carried him back out of the lab. Jann stood up and surveyed the devastation. The bodies of two geneticists lay dead along with one of Alban's cohort. "Two dead. That means there's only one still alive. We need to find him."

"Over here, have a look at this." Anika pointed to drops of blood on the ground. "Looks like one of them is injured. We just need to follow."

The trail led off towards the back of the cavern. "What's back there?" Jann whispered.

"The main research lab, where they did all the experimental work."

"Any way out?"

"There are metal stairs leading back up to the main colony area. It comes out near Vanji's living quarters."

THEY PASSED along by the experimentation rooms. Long tubular tanks filled with strange aquatic species. Flat rows of experimental flora, new strains of genetically modified plants for the colony gardens.

"Shhhh." Nills held a finger to his lips.

Jann listened to the silence, then she heard a clang of metal on metal.

"He's making for the stairs. Come, let's finish this."

But before they could move, the forlorn figure of the last geneticist moved out from behind a tall equipment rack. Behind him, Alban gripped his neck with one hand. In the other he held a grenade high in the air. The pin was removed. The only thing stopping it from detonating was his grip on the lever.

"Lower your weapons or I let go of this and take us all down."

"Alban, this is crazy. There's no way out."

"Oh yes there is. So just do it and step aside."

Nills was first to drop his weapon, then Jann, followed by Anika. Alban pushed the geneticist forward as he moved, and they let him pass, back into the research lab, turning around as he went.

"Back, move right back, as far as the wall."

They stepped back slowly until they were against the cave wall.

When Alban reached the center of the research lab he kicked the back of his captive's legs, and the geneticist collapsed to his knees on the floor. They could see him now taking off a shoulder bag and laying it down on a workbench.

"Oh shit," said Nills. "That's the bag with all the grenades Gizmo made."

"You know, Nills, I never really liked what happened to us up here. It's not what I had imagined when I signed up."

"You mean, when your alpha signed up."

"You see, that's what I'm talking about. Where does my alpha stop and me begin?" Ever think about that, Nills?"

"All the time, Alban. But we are what we are, we just need to get past it."

"Well I'm sorry, Nills. But I finally realized that I can't." Alban let go of the spring and dropped the live grenade into the bag. "I told you there was a way out."

"OH SHIT," was the last thing Jann heard before she was slammed against the cave wall and lost consciousness.

28

A NEW SOL

Nills moved through the Colony Two entrance cavern to the waiting rover. The mechanics working in the area waved to him as he passed. He nodded his acknowledgment. The colony was beginning to settle down in the weeks after the revolt. The seeds of a fragile peace were beginning to grow. Life would go on.

He stepped inside the machine and sat down in the cockpit. Xenon was already there, waiting.

"Ready to go, Nills?"

"Yeah, let's take it out, I hear it's a nice day outside."

Xenon took the controls and moved the rover through the main airlock and out onto the Martian surface. Nills was right, it was a nice day. A pale orb hung high in the sky, the air was clear, no wind to whip up the dust. Xenon looked up through the windscreen at the clear sky. "You think they're up there, watching us?"

Nills took a glance up, as if it was actually possible for him to spot a satellite flying past. "You better believe it. After all the coming and going, not to mention explosions on the planet's surface, they will have everything they can called into service. All trained on this very spot. NASA's deep space communications network is probably working overtime."

Xenon looked up again and gave the sky the one fingered salute. Nills laughed.

The hybrid leader had changed since his experience in the tank. All the hybrids had. Their uncanny ability to communicate by thought, far from being an evolutionary advantage, was in reality their Achilles heel. It had traumatized them to the point of despair. After the events of the recycling it took some time to get them out of their collective shell. Xenon was the one to do it. He was a different person now, with a different perspective. It was like some door had opened in his mind and he realized that the hybrids were a very fragile species. Their survival relied on the support and social cooperation of the betas. It took time for him to bring everybody around to this new reality. Some of the hybrids were still scarred, they would take longer. For a few, it would be never at all. But they would all help them as best they could.

"Do you have many memories of Earth?" Xenon asked.

"Yeah, sure. Although, technically I've never been there."

"It must be strange to walk out in the open, feel rain on your face, swim in an ocean of water."

"We all have memories of times on Earth, even you, Xenon. Anyway, our home is here. We need to make it our very own paradise."

They traveled in silence for a while and Nills reflected on the events that had brought them to this point.

The geneticists were all dead and the explosion in the labs had destroyed much of what they had created. It was certain that a considerable amount of their knowledge died with them, or was lost in the chaos. Still, they weren't without hope that what they needed could be salvaged, and at least the cave wall held the blast. A breach would have meant catastrophe, the end of human life on Mars.

Xenon broke his ruminations. "So what do think they're up to?

"Who?"

Xenon pointed skyward.

"We'll know soon enough, once we get to Colony One." They could already see its outline, and the massive biodome sparkled in the mid-sol sun. They rolled up to the facility and Xenon deftly reversed the rover up to the umbilical airlock. There was a satisfying clunk as the connection was made secure. Using this airlock meant that they had no need for bulky EVA suits, and made the trip a little easier.

When they stepped out, Becky and Gizmo were there

to greet them. Gizmo's arm had been repaired and the little robot was back to being 97.65% operational, as it put it. Quite what the remaining 2.35% was, nobody could fully understand. They walked through the connecting tunnel and into the main common room.

"Rachel's in the operations room, reviewing the facility schematics, if you're ready to have a look?"

The plan was to survey the derelict areas of Colony One to assess what would be required to repair those sections and bring them back online. Rachel and Becky had taken charge of the project and were eager to get started.

"Xenon, you go ahead. I'm just going to visit the biodome for a while."

"Sure." He nodded.

Nills walked through the short connecting tunnel, past the hydroponics, under the hanging vines and eventually found his way out onto the central dais. Sitting in a wicker recliner was Dr. Jann Malbec. She jumped up when she saw him come.

"Nills, you finally got here. Come, sit down." She walked over to the pond and pulled out a bottle of colony cider. "I've been saving this." She sat down and poured some glasses. "Here you go." They clinked. "To..." Jann thought for a second. "To Mars."

Nills raised his glass. "To Mars."

Jann had escaped the carnage in the labs with a gash on her head and a very sore body. Other than that she was okay. By the time order had been restored, and the population in Colony Two had come to terms with the new normal, she had decided to make the trip back. Nills stayed behind, promising to follow later when he was sure things had settled down. That was three weeks ago.

He sipped his drink. "So, any news from the ISA... from Earth?"

"We're front page news, have been for the last month. It's all out in the open."

"What do they know?"

"That's not really the problem, it's what people are speculating that's the problem."

"Is always is."

"What about Xenon, did you get any more of the story out of him?"

"A bit. From what he's told me, Vanji got frustrated with being consistently blocked by the council over his ambitions. So when he realized that you held the key to getting back to Earth, he did a deal with COM."

"VanHoff?"

"Yes. He had been communicating with them for a while, hatching a deal. They were going to give him anything he wanted, if he would come back. Xenon didn't know the details, just that they would take control of Colony Two and start a breeding program."

"Well, Earth thinks we hold the key to immortality, that we possess the elixir of life and they all want it now. The ISA are being sued to open up communications control with us. They're freaking out, they can't handle it."

"Well, that's their problem. We don't have to talk to anybody if we don't want to."

"Yes and no. Sure, we can switch off comms but that's not going to stop them coming here. I imagine that right now there are corporate boards meeting back on Earth, talking about how to raise money for a Mars mission. They are going to come, not just COM, but every space company and reckless adventurer."

"I don't suppose it would do any good to tell them we don't know anything."

"I already did. They don't believe me. They just think we're keeping it for ourselves." Jann sighed and sipped her drink.

"Nills, this could get very messy. The people that come will be non-state, well funded and probably well armed. Any so-called Outer Space Treaty laws that exist will be torn up and burned. They will fight each other for this knowledge, they will fight us for it and if we don't, or can't, give it to them they will simply experiment on us until they find it—or we're all dead. Make no mistake, Nills, a battle is coming. A battle for control of Mars."

They sat in silence for some time. Eventually Jann stood up. "But hey, it's not going to happen anytime soon, so let's enjoy the peace while we've got it." She stripped out of her jumpsuit, ran naked to the pond and dove in. Her head broke back up through the surface and she shook the water from her hair.

"So what are you waiting for?"

Nills gave a broad grin, stripped out of his own clothes and dove in beside her.

TO BE CONTINUED...

YOU CAN FIND the next book in the series, Colony Three Mars, here.

ALSO BY GERALD M. KILBY

You can find the next book in the series, Colony Three Mars, on Amazon.

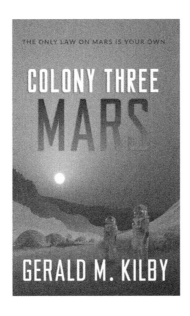

Now that the truth of the genetic experiments on Mars has been revealed, new missions are on their way to gain control of this extraordinary technology.

ABOUT THE AUTHOR

Gerald M. Kilby grew up on a diet of Isaac Asimov, Arthur C. Clark, and Frank Herbert, which developed into a taste for Iain M. Banks and everything ever written by Neal Stephenson. Understandable then, that he should choose science fiction as his weapon of choice when entering the fray of storytelling.

CHAIN REACTION is his first novel and is very much in the old-school techno-thriller style while his latest book series, **MOON BASE DELTA, COLONY MARS** and **THE BELT,** are all best sellers, topping Amazon charts for Hard Science Fiction and Space Exploration.

He lives in the city of Dublin, Ireland, in the same neighborhood as Bram Stoker and can be sometimes seen tapping away on a laptop in the local cafe with his dog Loki.

You can connect with G.M. Kilby at: www. geraldmkilby.com

youtube.com/@GeraldMKilbyAuthor

facebook.com/geraldmkilby

x.com/geraldmkilby

Made in the USA
Monee, IL
04 November 2024